Backlash

Ben Dalton, a gunfighter, arrives in Hawk's Bend hoping he has found a place where he can hang up his gun. Instead he steps into a feud about water rights between a farmer and a rancher. His hope of remaining out of the trouble goes up in smoke when he has to kill the rancher's hotheaded son to stop him raping Nora Wade, the farmer's wife.

Then there is Eli Bracken, the crooked marshal of Hawk's Bend, who has lined his pockets by doing the dead man's dirty deeds. Soured by the loss of a lucrative income he has every motive for killing Ben Dalton. Now the scene is set for a hellish showdown. But will Ben's gun skills see him through?

Backlash

RIO BLANE

A Black Horse Western

ROBERT HALE · LONDON

© James O'Brien 2003
First published in Great Britain 2003

ISBN 0 7090 7370 4

Robert Hale Limited
Clerkenwell House
Clerkenwell Green
London EC1R 0HT

Typeset by
Derek Doyle & Associates, Liverpool.
Printed and bound in Great Britain by
Antony Rowe Limited, Wiltshire

CHAPTER ONE

'Can't you read, boy?' Buck Cole boomed, his finger stabbing at the sign that read:

CIRCLE C DOMAIN
TRESPASSERS HANGED OR SHOT
ACCORDING TO PREFERENCE

Randy Wade cowered.

'No, sir,' he answered honestly, the boy's vague blue eyes mirroring his struggle to make sense of the men who had thundered into Bowie Creek.

' 'Course he can't, Pa,' Stryker Cole, Buck Cole's son sniggered. 'All that poor old Randy Wade's got inside his head is air.'

'Yipeeee!'

One of the men, Blackjack Ryan, an appellation earned by his fondness for the card game, and Stryker Cole's sidekick and willing accomplice in mayhem, tugged on his horse's reins, spreading the beast's mouth with the bit until the stallion's eyes went wild with pain. The horse reared up on its hindlegs. Ryan increased his pull on the reins and danced the horse towards Randy Wade, front legs flaying. The rearing horse forced the boy to throw himself aside.

The dim-witted youngster, already scared by Blackjack Ryan's antics, was completely unhinged and pitched headlong into the mud of the creek. The fish he had caught scattered from his grasp, and a couple of Circle C hands leaped from their horses to pound them to mush with their boots.

Tears burst from Randy Wade's eyes. Then his tearfulness was replaced by a stubborn, hot anger. He picked up a rock and threw it at one of the men. The rock grazed the man's head.

'Why, you scrambled-brain idiot!'

Buck Cole's boot shot out of his stirrup to shove the man back as he closed on the boy.

Stryker Cole said, 'Fair is fair, Pa. That rock could have done real damage to Andy's head.'

'More if it got him below the belt,' another rannie joked.

It was a joke that died a death under the injured man's furious glare and Buck Cole's critical gaze. The rancher frowned on lewdness. The Circle C boss addressed Randy Wade:

'Didn't your ma and pa tell you that this creek, being Circle C property, is off limits, boy?'

The stubbornness in the youngster's eyes became even more resolute.

'This ain't Circle C prop . . . prop . . . Whatever, Mr Cole.'

'That a fact, air-head,' Stryker Cole fumed, edging his horse close to Randy, his boot working free of his stirrup.

'Hold it, Stryker!' Buck Cole commanded.

'I don't believe that you're mollycoddling this cur, Pa,' the rancher's son growled. 'I reckon we should teach him a lesson.'

Andy Kennedy, the man on the receiving end of Randy Wade's rock, agreed.

'I reckon so too, Mr Cole.' His mean, pebble eyes burned holes in Randy Wade. 'Right now.'

'I'm boss of this outfit,' Buck Cole reminded the crew. 'There'll be no lessons taught. The Circle C doesn't harm kids.'

He addressed Randy Wade. This time his voice was soft and kindly.

'Didn't mean to scare you, boy. But you see, any day now new stock will be crowding into this creek. It'll be dangerous being around here. The Circle C needs the water. I've talked to your ma and offered her a fair price to add this creek to the Circle C. She turned me down. That leaves me with a real problem, son.'

'Ma said that as soon as Pa is on his feet again, he'll be needing the water from the creek for the farm, Mr Cole.'

Stryker Cole scoffed. 'Your pa has lung sickness. He ain't never going to get better.'

Randy Wade's blue eyes clouded over with

7

puzzlement. 'Ma said that Pa will be good as new pretty soon.'

Stryker Cole snorted. 'Your ma—'

'Shush, Stryker,' Buck Cole snapped. 'No call to make the boy fret. Fretting ain't good for him.'

Kennedy proffered his lariat. 'This is what's needed for that Wade brood, Mr Cole.'

The rancher withered the man with a look of scornful contempt.

Stryker Cole reminded his father: 'You hanged enough men in your time, Pa.'

Buck Cole agreed. 'Sure did. But they were men who deserved and needed hanging. Ned Wade was once a fine man and a good neighbour—'

'Ned Wade ain't the problem, Pa,' Stryker growled.

Buck Cole reacted angrily. 'You want to hang a woman?'

'She's a real thorn in our side, Pa,' Stryker said.

Blackjack Ryan leaned close to Stryker Cole and murmured in an aside: 'Thought you had other plans for Nora Wade, Stryker? Plans you'd need her breathing for.'

Buck Cole's look of contempt was transferred to Ryan, and was even more scornful. 'If you've got anything of value to say, let's all hear it, Ryan.'

Ryan, who enjoyed Stryker Cole's favour, reckoned he had no need to squirm.

'Ain't nothin' worth hearin', Mr Cole,' he answered cockily.

'What 'bout the boy, boss?' Kennedy questioned, taking courage from Blackjack Ryan's swaggering defiance. Kennedy's hand massaged his head. 'Is he goin' to get 'way scot free for this?'

Buck Cole said, 'You deserved what you got, Kennedy. Scaring the boy the way you did.'

Turning aside Kennedy muttered, 'It's this kinda shilly-shallyin's got the Circle C in trouble the way it is.'

Buck Cole's boot shot out and landed on Kennedy's back to pitch him forward into the creek.

'Don't like mumblers,' he snarled. The rancher's gaze shot to Blackjack Ryan. 'If a man's got something to say, then he should spit it out.'

Randy Wade, amused by Buck Cole's action, let go with a *hee-haw* that earned him Kennedy's malice.

'Some day, boy—'

'Some day nothing,' Buck Cole grated. 'Harm the boy and you'll damn well answer to me, Kennedy. Randy, you tell your folks that I'll be dropping by again soon to jaw again about selling me this creek.'

'Yes, sir,' Randy replied. 'Surely will. Soon as I get home.'

The rancher tossed a wide-eyed Randy Wade a silver dollar. 'I figure that that's a fair price for your fish.'

Randy cupped the dollar in his hand, fearing to avert his gaze lest the silver dollar vanished.

'Gee, thanks, Mr Cole.'

'You run along now. Give my best wishes to your folks, Randy.'

Randy Wade raced off in a stumbling gait, his eyes firmly fixed on the silver dollar.

The men were prepared to accept Buck Cole's admonishment of Kennedy for mouthing off. But rewarding Randy Wade raised their hackles. Stryker Cole spoke for them:

'That was a darn fool thing to do, Pa.'

Buck Cole glared at his son with whom he had a cold relationship, considering him to be a trouble-seeker when there was no good or just cause. The rancher's grey eyes swept the assembled riders. He growled:

'Any man who wants to ride out is free to leave. You'll get what's your due.'

Tension crackled. All eyes were on Stryker Cole. The stand-off dragged on, and might have developed in to outright defiance if another rider, a lanky dark-haired stranger, had not chosen then to put in an appearance.

'Who the hell are you?' Buck Cole wanted to know.

The stranger led his horse to the creek to drink, ignoring the rancher's demand.

'Are you deaf, stranger?' Stryker Cole asked. 'My pa asked you a question.'

'I heard,' the lanky man drawled.

'You going to answer?' Stryker Cole snarled. 'Or do I have to make you?'

'Maybe,' the stranger said. Now his bleak gaze

was rock-steady on Stryker Cole. 'And if you try, you'll come off worse.'

Stryker Cole leapt from his saddle and took up a fighting stance.

'You'll answer or I'll whup you to a standstill, mister.'

The lanky man smiled. 'Like I said. If you try—'

'I know what you said,' Stryker yelled. 'And you don't scare me none.'

'Then,' the stranger drawled, 'you're even dumber than that slow-witted boy you've been scaring.' His tone dropped an icy notch. 'I ain't no kid, fella.'

Stryker Cole choked with indignation. No one had ever spoken to him like that. Buck Cole reined in his son.

'Easy, Stryker,' he advised, seeing in the stranger a man he suspected was snake-spit quick with a gun.

'Listen,' the lanky visitor to the creek told Stryker Cole. 'The man's talking good sense.'

Defiantly, Stryker Cole spat. 'I make my own decisons, mister.'

The stranger returned: 'In that case, with a hot head like yours, you ain't going to be around for very long.'

'Long enough to teach you a lesson, smart mouth,' the rancher's son ranted.

The stranger looked to Buck Cole. Their eyes met challengingly.

'Your boy?' the stranger asked.

Buck Cole did not answer.

'Guess so,' the lanky man concluded. 'Same gait.'

'You talk to me, mister?' Stryker Cole demanded of the stranger.

'Don't take kindly to being ordered,' the stranger told Buck Cole, and warned: 'Pull on your boy's reins, mister.'

Stryker Cole scoffed. 'Don't you pay no heed, Pa,' he bragged 'I can take him any time I want.'

'Ain't so,' the stranger told Buck Cole. His gaze was steady on the rancher. 'And I reckon you know that.'

During Stryker Cole's challenge, one of the Circle C hands had edged behind the stranger, and this was the reason for Stryker Cole's bravado. It was the kind of sneaky ploy that irked Buck Cole. But he'd let it go unchallenged. He had no choice. Because he had no doubt that his only son and heir to all he possessed had worked himself into a bind that would prove mighty difficult to wriggle out of.

'This over and done with?' the stranger asked Buck Cole. 'All I need is to water my horse, fill my canteen, rustle up some grub, and I'll be making tracks.'

The lanky visitor's dismissal of Stryker Cole incensed him. He screamed:

'You settle with me, you bastard!'

'Don't like profanity,' the stranger intoned.

'That a fact?' Stryker Cole snorted. 'BASTARD!'

12

The stranger dropped his horse's reins, and settled his stance. His shoulders heaved in a weary sigh.

'Guess it ain't over with yet,' he groaned.

Buck Cole said, 'Are you loco, stranger? There's ten of us.'

'Yeah,' the stranger drawled with a hint of Texas in his tones, 'but,' his eyes locked with the rancher's, 'only one of your boy.'

Buck Cole swallowed hard.

'You want to risk his funeral?' the stranger asked, his tone hollow. The rancher was weighing up the options when the stranger said, 'That creeper behind won't help any.'

With Stryker Cole's sneaky backup rumbled, the threat to his son became too great for Buck Cole to risk. Though he knew that the stranger's challenge and his backing-off would be the talk of the range and the town, too, he did not have a choice. Maybe the stranger was all wind. But maybe, too, he was as fast as lightning.

If there was one thing Buck Cole had learned early in the building of the Circle C, it was that backing off was not the way to do things in cow country. And that meant that in the future – and the not too distant future at that, he would have to deal with the lanky stranger who had dared to challenge Circle C surpremacy.

He wished that Stryker was as quick with his brain as with his gun. That way he would not have to constantly clean up the trouble he got himself into. But a man planted his seed and hoped for the best. Sometimes he didn't get what he hoped for.

'Take your water and get out!' Buck Cole told the stranger.

'Pa,' Stryker Cole whined, humiliated for the second time in as many minutes.

'Saddle up,' the rancher ordered his son.

Eager to ingratiate himself with Stryker Cole (who, with Buck Cole's health getting ropy, would be the Circle C boss soon), the man who had edged behind the stranger went for his gun. His hand had not got anywhere near the .45 before his chest exploded, and he was blasted back into the willows edging the creek.

Quick as a lizard's tongue, the stranger's gun swung to cover Stryker Cole and any other man who fancied his chances. A cold sweat broke on Buck Cole's back. He had seen fast guns before, but never anyone as fast as the lanky stranger.

'It's over with, mister,' the rancher chanted.

The stranger's brown, angry eyes scanned the gathering.

'Wow!' mumured a goggle-eyed Randy Wade.

Having seen the lanky stranger ride into the creek on his way out, he had been intrigued by his low-slung, thonged six-gun. He had hidden in the trees on a knoll overlooking the creek, curious as to what would come of this confrontation between him and the Circle C crew.

Now he knew.

'In that case . . .' The stranger slid his pistol

back into the well-worn holster, polished to a sheen no doubt by the gun's frequent use.

The Circle C riders splashed off along the creek. Randy did not budge, standing in awe of what he had witnessed.

'It'll rain soon, boy,' the stranger told Randy. 'Go on home now.'

Randy leapt up from his crouched position, surprised by the stranger's knowing that he was watching.

'Yes, mister,' Randy said, and ran off. Some way off, at what he considered to be a safe distance to escape if the stranger got as tetchy with him as he had with Stryker Cole, Randy Wade asked breathlessly, 'What's your name, mister?'

The lanky stranger answered: 'Dalton. Ben Dalton, son.'

Randy's eyes popped and his jaw hit his chest. 'Really, mister?'

'Really, son,' Ben Dalton confirmed.

'Gosh!'

Randy ran helter-skelter. Ben Dalton, ace gunfighter was in the territory, and he was the only one who knew.

CHAPTER TWO

Still some way off, Randy hollered excitedly, 'Ma!'

Hanging out the washing, Nora Wade was alarmed by her son's shout. She dropped the clothes-basket she was holding and raced to meet her breathless son.

'What is it, Randy?'

She checked him worriedly for any sign of injury.

'B – b . . .'

'Take your time and get your breath back,' his mother advised. And when he was calmed she asked: 'Now, what is it?'

Ready to leap from their sockets, Randy Wade's blue eyes danced with excitement.

'Ben Dalton's down at Bowie Creek,' he blurted.

Ned Wade had come from the cabin, the short journey stealing his breath from lungs that were past their best.

'Ben Dalton?' Nora questioned Randy.

'Yes, Ma,' the boy exclaimed. 'And he's even faster than folk said he was, too.'

'Faster?'

'Yep.'

'There was gunplay?'

'What's all the excitement about, Nora?'

Nora Wade waved impatiently at her husband. 'Just a minute, Ned.'

'Killed a man,' Randy stated bluntly.

Randy shrugged. 'Don't know his name, Ma. One of Buck Cole's men.' Disbelief spread across Nora Wade's windblown face and into her hazel eyes.

'Wow!' Randy sighed. 'Fast. Real fast, Ma.'

Nora Wade set aside her surprise. Her immediate worry being any fall-out from the events at the creek coming their way, she scanned the horizon for any sign of trouble. Finding none, she gathered Randy to her and hurried back to the cabin.

'Well,' Ned Wade demanded tetchily. 'Ain't no one going to—'

'Ben Dalton's down at Bowie Creek,' Nora interjected.

Ned Wade's doubt was stark. 'Ben Dalton?'

'Randy saw him,' Nora said.

Wade's doubt became even more stark.

'Jawed with him too, Pa,' Randy said. 'Ain't that somethin'?' The boy's eyes lit up with new excitement, and he drew an imaginary gun. 'Pow! Pow! Fast!'

'That a fact, boy.' Wade snorted, shaking his black-thatched head, his eyes rife with amusement.

'So what does this Dalton fella look like?'

Ned Wade had once seen Ben Dalton on a trip to Dodge City, and his crowbait visage was not easily forgotten.

'Well . . . .' Randy began, his brow furrowing in thought.

'I'm waiting, boy,' Wade grumbled, as his son's time to gather his scrambled thoughts lengthened.

'Give him a chance, Ned,' Nora Wade rebuked her husband.

'Where did I get such an airhead boy from?' Wade snapped.

'He's your seed,' Nora said.

Ned Wade scowled. 'No need to keep on reminding me,' he growled. 'Ain't it enough to have to look at him ev'ry day I draw breath.'

As he struggled to marshal his thoughts in to some kind of order, the fiery exchange between his parents passed Randy Wade by.

'Looks like that scarecrow we've got in the field, Pa,' he announced.

Ned Wade's eyes shot Randy's way.

'Tall. Real tall,' Randy said. 'Eyes that . . .' Randy shivered. 'And one of them things . . .' He indicated his throat, frustrated at his inability to finish his description of the gunfighter.

'An Adam's apple?' Nora suggested.

Randy nodded his head adamantly. 'A real big one, Ma.'

'I'll be . . . .'

Nora and Randy Wade looked to Ned Wade,

whose doubt had fled.

'Dalton?' Nora asked her husband.

'I reckon,' Wade confirmed.

Nora Wade's worry raced back. 'A gunfighter. Buck Cole must have . . .' Then Nora recalled what Randy had said about Dalton killing a Cole wrangler. She questioned him closely. 'Randy, you said that Ben Dalton shot a Circle C hand, right?'

He nodded vigorously, and again drew his imaginary pistol. 'Pow! Fast!'

'Then Buck Cole could not have hired him,' Nora reasoned.

'Prob'ly just passing through and a Cole cur riled him,' Ned Wade suggested. He hunched his shoulders. 'One thing's for sure though . . .'

'What's that?' Nora asked.

'Ben Dalton ain't as fast with his brain as he is with his gun. Killing a Cole hand will have bought him a hornet's nest of trouble.'

'Ma,' Randy piped up, 'I near forgot. Mr Cole said to tell you and pa that he'll be calling round to talk about selling him the creek.'

'We've already talked,' Nora stated brusquely. 'There's nothing more to be said.'

'Maybe . . .'

Nora Wade's angry glance stalled her husband's words.

'We'll be needing that water, Ned, when you're back on your feet.'

Ned Wade held his tongue. There was no point in telling his wife that he would never again be *back on his feet*, that with every passing day his lungs were getting tighter and his breath shorter. She had closed her mind to his sickness, and there was nothing he or anyone could say to make her face the inevitable.

'Mr Cole said that the creek was already his, Ma,' Randy Wade said.

Nora scowled. 'Is that so. Well, it isn't! And,' her scowl deepened, 'it never will be.'

Ned Wade had tried to talk to his wife about the future. Buck Cole was offering a good price for Bowie Creek; money that would be sorely needed when he was gone. It was foolish of Nora to hold steadfastly to a dream that had turned sour when his lungs gave out. But there was no shifting her belief that one day the farm they had started together, in what seemed an age ago now, would amount to something. Even as late as the evening before Nora had been dreaming her dreams, and there was no getting through to her that shortly he wouldn't be around.

'Go inside the house with Pa, Randy,' Nora instructed.

'Where're you headed?' Wade called after her.

'To Bowie Creek, of course. To see this Ben Dalton with my own eyes.'

'Ben Dalton's a killer, Nora,' her husband cautioned.

'Once heard that he only killed those needing killing, Ned,' Nora called back.

'He's a gunfighter,' Ned Wade emphasized.

'And therefore, no gentleman.'

'He was once a lawman, too,' Nora reminded her husband. 'As for being a gentleman, well, I can't say until I meet him, now can I.'

'Nora,' he shouted after her, but knew that he was wasting what little breath he had.

Randy Wade was drawing his imaginary gun every second now, shooting down imaginary men left right and centre, yelping time and time again: 'Pow! Pow! Fast!'

'Get inside the house,' Ned Wade scolded.

Randy cowered. He had seen his father's rages of late and was at a loss to understand why he had so suddenly fallen out of favour with his pa. Seeing the naked fear in his son's eyes, Ned Wade was filled with self-loathing. His sickness had made him short-tempered. While Nora understood, Randy could not. Instinctively, he drew Randy to him. Nowdays he was critical of his boy's foolishness. But before his shortcomings had become obvious, he had been the proudest man in the valley. He just could not understand how two healthy parents could have a boy with scrambled brains. The Reverend Bland, in Hawk's Bend, had talked about the will of God and all that. But it made no difference to Ned Wade. He had long ago stopped believing in God.

Wade's constant worry nowadays was, what would become of his family when he was no longer around to care for them. Not, he thought bitterly, that he was caring for them now. As his sickness debilitated him more and more, Nora's workload had steadily increased. A proud man, becoming daily more and more dependent, his self-loathing increased. And it hurt him to see the radiant woman he had married become prune-like with exhaustion.

More than once he had been tempted to use his gun on himself and free Nora from her burden. His lack of courage added to his self-loathing. As he returned to the house, he began to think that by some strange twist of fate Ben Dalton's arrival in the valley would somehow bring the resolution needed.

CHAPTER THREE

Drawing near to Bowie Creek, Nora Wade caught the whiff of frying bacon and brewing coffee on the southerly breeze. The combination sharpened her hunger pangs. With Ned Wade disabled for over a year and little coming in, there had been sparse and even downright hungry days in the Wade house. That very day was one such day.

Nora slowed as she neared the creek, to watch the lanky man preparing his meal. Now that she had arrived, Nora wondered why she had come. What had she hoped to gain by meeting Ben Dalton? She supposed that when she had set out, she had had the idea somewhere in the back of her mind that she would ask Dalton for his help in dealing with the Coles, particularly that cur Stryker Cole. Buck Cole was a man of great ambition who saw the Circle C eventually spreading from one county border to the next, but he had in the main made the Circle C what it was by fair dealing. Stryker Cole preferred to settle things with a gun.

Of course there had been wild and lawless

times in the past when the gun and rope ruled the range. Back then Buck Cole had not been faint-hearted in dealing out rough and quick justice when throat-slitting desperadoes roamed the countryside. There had been a need for swift justice then. But times had changed. Law had been established in the territory, most of it fair and good. However, there were men who sported a star whose only purpose in doing so was their own self-enrichment. And the curse of tainted law such as they had in Hawk's Bend in the person of Eli Bracken was a curse greater than no law at all.

Buck Cole did not count Bracken among his friends. But that did not hold true for Stryker Cole. The rancher's son and Eli Bracken had a devil's pact. Bracken, in return for Stryker Cole's largesse, legalized his wrongdoing, be it murder or simple rowdyism. With Cole senior's hold on the Circle C slipping by the day, Bracken did more and more of Stryker's dirty chores in the hope that when Stryker finally became the boss of the Circle C, his need for his services would be greater and consequently so would his largesse.

Bracken had pulled every dirty legal trick he knew to add Bowie Creek to the Circle C, but up to now the curse of an honest attorney, Augustus Bramble, working for Nora Wade, had spiked all his efforts. Eventually it would come down to simply grabbing the creek by arranging an accident for the Wades. He had not set a price for that particular piece of skulduggery, yet. But when he did, it would not come cheap.

No fool, Buck Cole knowing the lengths to which Stryker might go to make Bowie Creek part of the Circle C, had upped his offer to Nora Wade time and again to avoid what, shortly, when the new herd arrived on Circle C grass, would be an emergency.

'Maybe,' he had stated on his last visit to the Wade homestead to make his latest offer for the creek, 'you'd be well advised to accept my offer, Nora. Before lead starts flying. I'm a patient man, but . . . Well, Stryker's young and in a hurry. Like I was, I guess.'

'I don't know how many times I have to tell you this, Buck,' Nora had responded testily. 'Bowie Creek is not for sale.'

Buck Cole had stormed off, warning darkly: 'Soon I'll have more cows than I'll have water for, Nora. And I don't aim to be burying any from thirst!'

When he left, Ned Wade had grumbled: 'Don't my view count 'round here no more, Nora?'

Her anger still up, Nora had brusquely replied, 'You've got a mouth to speak with, Ned.'

'What would be the point, Nora,' he had said, the fire suddenly gone out of him. 'When everyone sees you as the future and me as the damn past.' Moved, Nora had gone to hold her husband, but he had shrugged off her embrace, and growled, 'Keep your damn pity!'

Of late, Ned Wade had taken to sleeping alone. 'Easier,' was his explanation to Nora when she asked about his departure from her bed. 'Lying with you is too hard, Nora. A man's needs takes a lot of breath, which I ain't got any more.'

It was a fact. The last time they had made love Ned had turned purple, and for a while Nora had feared that he had used up all the breath he had, that there simply was no more left. But it was not easy lying alone. A woman had needs, too. But no one ever thought a woman had needs, and in the times that they were in the expression of those needs in word or deed would bring shock to the community and ostracism for the woman.

Shocked, Nora Wade found that she was watching Ben Dalton as a man and not as the gunfighter who had roused her curiosity. He was no oil-painting for sure, but there was a masculinity about him that lit fires in Nora that she thought had long burned out.

Ben Dalton was as Randy had described. If one imagined a couple of tufts of straw poking out from under his hat, he was a lot like the scarecrow in their field out back. His lankiness was perilously close to beanpole, and his hollow cheeks would get him trouble-free on to a mortician's table. But he sat, and, Nora figured, would move with the grace and swiftness of a cougar if the need arose.

He poured another cup of coffee from the shiny coffee-pot (she had never seen a coffee-pot shine so, which showed Dalton to be a tidy and probably a proud man too) while the bacon fried. Nora's hollow innards quaked at the smell of the bacon as it reached golden crispness.

Ben Dalton was a man at peace with himself, and Nora envied him. It had been a long time since she had had peace, and the future held out little prospect of improvement in her fortunes. In fact, with Ned failing more every day, and the Circle C angling to axe the creek, things could not get much worse.

'You're welcome to join me if you want, ma'am.'

Ben Dalton's invitation stunned Nora. How did he know she was there? She had taken the greatest care in making her approach. And how did he know that it was a woman watching him?

'Of course,' the gunfighter added, 'if you just want to sit and watch that's allright, too.'

Hot colour flooded Nora Wade's cheeks.

Ben Dalton continued: 'Can't rightly say that I like being watched, though.' He chuckled. 'Even by a woman.' The gunfighter elaborated: 'Known some women in my time who were more danger-ous than a mountain cat and more poisonous than a rattler.'

'I'm neither!' Nora replied starchily.

'Glad to hear that, ma'am. It'll help the bacon go down a mite easier.'

Mad at being rumbled, Nora clambered unheedingly down the steep bank. Half-way down her foot caught on a root, and the remainder of her descent was completed in a topsy-turvy tumble, until she landed next to Ben Dalton not knowing which end was up.

Smiling wryly, Dalton commented: 'I just bet you're one fine dancing lady, ma'am.'

'Go to hell, Ben Dalton!' Nora spat.

The gunfighter was instantly alert.

'How come you know my name?' he asked with quiet suspicion.

'My boy told me.'

'Your boy?' Then, recollecting Randy Wade. 'The . . .' He bit off his words.

Seeing the formation of the word on Dalton's lips, Nora Wade finished for him:

'Simpleton.'

'Sorry, ma'am. Didn't mean to give offence.'

'No offence, Mr Dalton. It's a fact,' Nora stated brusquely. 'Randy is short some marbles, but I wouldn't change him for any other.'

'I'm sure you wouldn't, ma'am,' Ben Dalton said.

He considered Nora Wade. Behind the pallor of hunger and exhaustion, Dalton saw the ghost of a very beautiful woman.

'How did you know you were being watched by a woman, Mr Dalton?'

'That'll be Ben, ah . . . ?'

'Nora.'

'Nice handle. Knew a Nora once. Almost married her.' His brown eyes were warm with memories.

'Why didn't you?'

30

Ben Dalton gave Nora's question deep thought, and concluded: 'You know, Nora, damned if I know.'

'You didn't answer my question, Ben.'

Nora was surprised how easy his name slipped from her tongue, and how much she liked the sound of it.

'Scent, Nora.' Hellfire-red colour shot to Nora Wade's cheeks. The gunfighter stated matter-of-factly, 'In my line of work smell can often save a man's life. For example, Indians smell different from white men. Negros different from Mex gents, too. And a woman . . .'

He grinned and, despite fighting it, Nora could not stem the tide of warmth that flooded through her.

'Well,' Dalton said ponderously, 'a woman's scent is very special, Nora.'

Fretting her dark hair with busy fingers, Nora said, 'Stop this foolish talk right now, Ben Dalton.'

After a moment, Dalton offered: 'Coffee, if you want. Bacon, too.'

Nora glanced at the crisply curling bacon in the frying-pan. Her mouth watered. But her pride kicked in.

'Ain't hungry.'

'Sure about that, Nora?'

'I'm sure.'

'Hate to eat alone,' the gunfighter said.

'On the trail you must eat alone a lot?'

'Yes, that I do. So when I have someone to share

with it makes it all the sweeter an experience for me.' He proffered the pan of bacon. 'I'd be obliged if you'd join me.'

Nora closed her eyes on tasting the juicy bacon, giving her total concentration to savouring its salty tang. It had been a long while since bacon had been on the menu of the Wade household.

'Thank you, Ben.'

Ben Dalton had heard his name spoken by many women. But if he lived to be a hundred he knew that he would never again hear it in quite the same way that Nora Wade had spoken it.

'Have some more,' he invited, on seeing Nora lick her lips.

'I wouldn't want to—'

'Plenty more of the same in my war chest,' Dalton assured her.

She smiled. 'Well, in that case . . .'

He had lied. His war chest was leaner than it had ever been. Tired of continuous challenges by young tyros who wanted to make a fast reputation, he had been avoiding towns as much as was possible, only visiting when supplies hit rock bottom. That was his purpose now in heading into Hawk's Bend. His visit would be brief and, he hoped, trouble free. In truth he had grown weary of being on the trail, and of late had had a hankering to settle down. He had hopes that Hawk's Bend might offer him refuge; a place where he could hang up his gun. But on the evidence so far, it looked unlikely. Nowdays, he viewed each new town as a possible haven. However, it seemed he was destined to be on the move, until some town would become his final resting place.

He chewed long and hard on the bacon he had in his mouth to allow Nora eat her fill. He emptied the dregs of his cup. He poured fresh coffee and handed it to Nora.

'You'll be needing that to wash down the salt.'

Nora thought that for a gunfighter, Ben Dalton was a mighty hospitable man. And even more important, a very charitable and kind man. He had made a big play of going off his grub to save her feelings, which marked him down as a man who did not gloat over another body's misfortune.

The last smidgen of taste sucked from the last shred of bacon, Nora confessed: 'Times have been hard, Ben. Really hard.'

'Luck run out?'

Nora said, wearily, 'And it looks like it's never coming back neither.'

'It goes round,' Ben Dalton said. 'Just takes time to make the return journey, Nora.' His gaze trapped hers. 'Would these hard times have something to do with the men who wanted to run me off?'

'That would be Buck Cole and his boy Stryker.'

'Cole's got the meat on him of comfortable living.'

'He's the biggest rancher in the territory. It would take a fine horse to ride from one boundary to the other of the Circle C.' Then, bitterly, 'And that isn't enough for him!'

'They say much covets more,' Dalton drawled.

'And still more.'

Shrewdly, Dalton observed: 'This creek's got a good flow to it. Clean, too. Lots of range needs lots of clean water. This your water, Nora?'

'Yes.'

'You ranch, too?'

'No. Ned and me farm. Or at least we did before . . .'

'Before what?' the gunfighter prompted.

'Ned Wade is not a well man. Lung sickness. I've done my best, but . . .' Nora shrugged hopelessly.

'Fatal?' Dalton asked bluntly. 'The lung sickness?'

'It's shaping up that way.'

'A man with lung sickness needs clean, dust-free air, Nora. You should head for Montana. Sweetest air there is.'

'Ned couldn't make the trip, Ben. Nowdays not five minutes passes without a coughing fit.'

'Sounds like consumption.'

'Guess it is. Or worse.'

'Has he seen a doctor?'

'The sawbones in Hawk's Bend. Keeps giving him some foul-smelling concoction to take. Doesn't do anything for the coughing, but it's powerful for the bowels.'

Despite the gloominess of the topic under discussion, the gunfighter laughed. His apology on seeing Nora's glare was instant.

'Sorry, Nora.'

Her anger faded, and a frail, sad smile crossed her lips. 'Ned will have the cleanest innards of any corpse there ever was.'

Again, Ben Dalton's shrewdness showed through. 'My guess would be that this fella Cole wants this creek.'

'He does.'

'Made you an offer? Or is it his intention to just grab it?'

'Buck Cole made a more than fair offer.'

'And?'

'And I don't want to sell. When Ned gets back on his feet again, we'll need this water ourselves. We've got plans to irrigate the south pasture.' She drew up short on seeing Ben Dalton's quizzical gaze. 'Maybe,' she said wistfully, 'a miracle will happen, Ben.'

'Believe in miracles, Nora?'

Gaze steady on Ben Dalton, Nora said, 'Maybe I'm beginning to, Ben.'

Dalton waited, allowing Nora Wade to pick her own time to put in to words what was in her head. She did.

'Would you help Ned and me, Ben?'

'Help you?' he hedged. 'How?'

'To fight Buck Cole, of course,' Nora said impatiently.

The gunfighter held up his hands. 'Whoa, now, Nora. I'm just passing through. Trouble is not on my agenda.'

Nora's shoulders slumped. 'I guess there are no

35

miracles after all.'

'Want my advice?'

'I know what your advice will be,' Nora said sharply. 'Accept Buck Cole's offer and get out.'

He nodded. 'He'll take the creek anyway. Like it or not. You might as well make the best deal you can, while you still have a chance.'

The sound sense of Ben Dalton's reasoning was not new to Nora Wade. Buck Cole had already made the same argument, as had Ned Wade, and she knew the wisdom of packing up and moving on. However, by doing that she would be giving up on the dream which she and Ned had shared when they settled in the valley six years previously. After accompanying her husband through a variety of dead-end jobs and misfortunes, Nora saw golden days ahead. Buck Cole had even helped Ned build the cabin and, uncharacteristic for a cattleman, did not object to a sodbuster as a neighbour.

But they had soon learned that their stay in the valley was conditional on their keeping their farming activities down to not much more than a cabbage patch. When Ned had begun fencing off some free range, Buck Cole had changed his tune.

'You're ploughing good range, Wade. Won't stand for that,' he had angrily proclaimed. 'I'll look on this as a mistake. You just let the grass grow back.'

Ned Wade had put in back-breaking work to prepare the ground to sow a crop of maize, and he was in no humour to listen to Circle C dictation.

He defied Buck Cole and grew his crop of maize, only to have it burned by Stryker Cole.

'Don't agree with what Stryker did,' Buck Cole had apologized on a visit to the farm to pay compensation for the loss of the crop, 'but being a cattleman, I can understand his anger at having good grass country ploughed up.'

He had put a pouch of silver dollars on the table.

'That should about cover your loss, Wade,' he had told Ned. 'And I hope that this foolishness is over and done with now.'

Ned, his spirits low, had let Nora respond to Buck Cole, and a fiery rebuff it had been. She took his dollars and flung them back in his face.

'You'll need your dollars to pay for Stryker's defence. He'll need a good lawyer to keep him from rotting in jail.'

'Defence?' Buck Cole bellowed. 'No Cole is going to jail on the say-so of a dirt farmer!'

'We'll see about that,' Nora spat back.

Buck Cole had left, his beefy shoulders shaking with laughter. There and then Nora had ridden into Hawk's Bend, certain that Stryker Cole would be made account for his actions. A couple of seconds after meeting Eli Bracken, she fully understood Buck Cole's laughing departure.

'You want me to arrest and charge Stryker Cole for burning your maize crop. Is that so, ma'am?' Bracken had asked, eyes wide with astonishment, and looking at Nora as if he had a lunatic on his hands. 'Is this some kind of joke, Mrs Wade?'

'You're the sheriff,' Nora had argued hotly. 'Stryker Cole committed a crime. It's your duty to act.'

By then Bracken's deputy was guffawing fit to bring on a hernia, while Eli Bracken was struggling to keep a straight face.

'Ma'am,' Bracken said, 'let me explain that in these parts a Cole does what he pretty much pleases. Buck or Stryker.'

'Arrest Stryker Cole,' the deputy hee-hawed. 'That's real funny, ma'am.'

On leaving the sheriff's office, Nora saw Stryker Cole swaggering from the saloon with a couple of cronies in tow. Probably the same ones who had helped him burn the maize crop. Nora cut straight across the street from the sheriff's office to the saloon, marched on to the porch, and slapped Stryker Cole's face. She was back on board her horse and heading out of town before the shock of what she had dared do registered. But she knew that her impetuous action had been unwise, and a hornet's nest had been stirred.

And so it proved to be.

The clatter of cooking-utensils as Ben Dalton packed up broke Nora Wade's reverie.

'I have some savings that I was keeping for seed,' she said hopefully. 'Not much, but . . .'

The gunfighter's impassiveness stalled her offer.

'Nora,' he said, 'you can't win against an outfit

like the Circle C. And for me to take your money and let you think that I'd make a difference, would be plain dishonesty.'

'Dishonest?' Nora spat. 'You're a killer. What's a little dishonesty compared to murder?'

A brief anger lit Ben Dalton's eyes, but he let go of it. Solemnly, he said, 'I've never killed a man just for the pleasure of killing him. All the men I drew against came looking for me, and wouldn't listen to reason. And,' he emphasized, 'I never hire out my gun.'

Stiffly, he finished: 'Now, if you'll excuse me, Nora. I'll be on my way.'

Ben Dalton mounted up. He rode out of Bowie Creek, leaving Nora Wade's hopes of hiring his gun in tatters. In her despair, for the first time, the fight gone out of her, Nora thought about accepting Buck Cole's offer.

CHAPTER FOUR

Stryker Cole stormed from the ranch house, rattling the windows in their frames with the ferocious slam of the front door. Fuming after the incident at Bowie Creek, he had confronted his father about pulling his reins but had got short shrift.

'While I'm around,' Buck Cole had unequivocally told his son, 'things at the Circle C will be done my way. Understood?'

'I'm not just another hand,' Stryker had argued. 'I'm your son.'

'All the more reason for you to obey me,' the rancher had flung back. 'It ain't right that you should be bucking my every order Stryker, in front of the men.'

'And it ain't right that you should be siding against me neither, Pa,' Stryker had spat.

Grim-faced, the rancher had answered; 'Then don't give me cause to, boy.'

'I'm not a boy!'

On that angry riposte, Stryker Cole had stormed out of the house.

'I haven't said you could leave,' Buck Cole had uselessly bellowed after his departing son.

'I ain't asking your permission for what I do, Pa,' the furious Stryker had hurled back. 'Not any more!'

Buck Cole went to the drawing-room window to watch Stryker stalk off across the yard to the stables, his anger replaced by worry. He had let his anger match his son's, and that always made for a bad outcome. A gap had opened up between him and Stryker which he did not know how to bridge. Each new day seemed to sour their relationship further. Buck Cole longed for the days when Stryker and he had been close as peas in a pod. But, of late, Stryker had more and more gone against his wishes, choosing the company of men whom Buck Cole would not allow in the house. Ranch hands the likes of Blackjack Ryan and Andy Kennedy, and an assortment of town dregs had become Stryker's companions. Ryan and Kennedy he should have run off the range a long time ago. Now, should he attempt to do so, he'd run the risk of losing Stryker too. Particularly, Ryan had got inside Stryker's head and planted his poison, and Buck Cole feared that should he confront Ryan, he'd suffer the humiliation of Stryker's siding with him. But more important, he'd run the risk of Stryker riding off into a badman's future with Blackjack Ryan. He had employed many Irishmen over the years of building the Circle C. Some had been good, honest workers; some had been lazy layabouts; others had been nothing but trouble. But of them all, Blackjack Ryan was one Irishman he wished he had never set eyes on.

Like most Irishmen, Ryan had a silken tongue that could turn a dirty deed into a saintly cause. He had filled Stryker Cole's head with tall tales and false promises. To his shame, Buck Cole had stood by while Ryan spun his yarns and fairytales and planted his poison until, now, he had Stryker mesmerized.

On the ride back to the ranch, he had given over his time to thinking about the man who had displayed nerves of steel back at Bowie Creek, and a dark thought had taken root. He had never favoured the use of a fast gun to extend the Circle C boundaries, and it pained him now to have to countenance it. But Nora Wade's stubborn refusal to sell Bowie Creek to him was, he reckoned, the root cause of the trouble between him and Stryker.

If that problem were resolved . . . .

Buck could not place the blame for his son's fiery approach to the solving of the problem on anyone's shoulders but his own. As a boy Stryker had seen him solve problems in a no-nonsense fashion. But that was when a man had to make his own law in a lawless land. At a time when a man had to make his own rules, or go under.

Times had changed. Law and order had come to the territory. He had been one of the prime movers in making it happen. Of course, there were some lawmen like Eli Bracken, the sheriff of

Hawk's Bend, who were partial to palm-greasing. The right amount could make them go deaf, dumb and blind. And Bracken, a particularly obnoxious and underhanded version of the species, was not averse to doing another man's dirty deeds if the price was right.

Some seemingly intractable problems for the Circle C had, of late, fortuitously resolved themselves. Buck Cole did not want to believe that Stryker's friendliness with Eli Bracken was a factor in their resolution. But he feared that if a US marshal were to become involved in matters, palm-greasing would not be an option to avoid trouble or justice.

There was no forgetting the way Jake Wright's boy, Frank, had been hauled off to a gallows and hanged for lynching a horse-thief – something he had watched his pa do time and again before law and order arrived.

In the days when the range was raw and the land rawer still, rustlers and horse-thieves could grab a man's entire herd. So there was little sympathy for them when they were caught. Over in the next county the same fate befell another rancher as had Frank Wright when, in a dispute over water rights with a sodbuster, he shot the farmer.

There was a time when shootings and hangings were the order of the day; when men had to take a stand or be hounded out. That time was past. Now disputes had to be settled by legal wrangling rather than lead or rope antics. And, try as hard as he might, he had not been able to get that fact into Stryker's hot head. Whenever he tried, Stryker's answer was always the same.

'Cole men solve their own problems, Pa. I see no reason for change just because a couple of out-of-territory marshals are poking their noses in.'

Eli Bracken had also warned Stryker Cole about changing times. But the Hawk's Bend sheriff had not pushed the rancher's son too hard. He'd be a fool to upset a pocket-filler like Stryker Cole. The slippery sheriff kept a couple of packed valises at the ready should a US marshal put in an appearance. Plans to spend his ill-gotten gains in new surroundings were well advanced. But he wasn't ready to leave town just yet. Trouble was coming to the boil between the Circle C and the Wades over Bowie Creek. Maybe the shysters might find a way to swindle Ned and Nora Wade out of the creek, but he was counting on more traditional methods being needed to secure the water which the Circle C needed. He'd keep his gun well oiled, in readiness for the kind of whacking great final payment from Stryker Cole which he was anticipating.

CHAPTER FIVE

His anger ferocious, Stryker Cole rode his horse to a standstill, drawing rein only when his mount's legs were spent and pushing the horse was dangerous. As a youngster he had been thrown from a tired horse, and ever since had had a fear of it happening again. He dismounted and sat restlessly on a boulder, rolled a smoke, and took to pondering about heading over to the Wade homestead for a showdown. He slid his six-gun from its holster, and spun the gun's chamber.

'This would solve the problem fast, and for good.'

Stryker Cole considered the gun. The sun reflected mesmerically off the barrel. A black resolve seeped through him. His light blue eyes, a perfect match for his fair locks, became fierce with the killing lust building in him. He sprang off the boulder.

'Wades,' he snarled. 'You've had your own damn way for too long!'

He mounted up, and was about to make tracks

for the Wade homestead when he spotted Nora Wade making her way home from Bowie Creek. Stryker Cole's mouth went sand-dry. His heart thumped in his chest. The blood rushed through his veins. A fire of fierce intensity sprang to life in his groin. A dark and terrible need overrode his reason. Demons awakened in him, and he became a driven man: driven by the hellish desire to possess Nora Wade.

He checked the countryside around. It was as deserted as the moon. A greasy sweat oozed from Stryker Cole's pores. His mind filled with the forbidden pleasures of the dark deed which was ripening in his head.

He swung his horse. Nora Wade's direction home would take her along a tree-shaded trail. If he was quick he could reach it ahead of her. There was that really dark stretch, where the trees touched and almost completely cut out the light. That was where he would wait for her.

Ben Dalton sat his horse uneasily. Since he had left the creek his mind had not been at rest. Nora Wade had strangely disturbed him, and not only in the normal way that such a comely woman upset a man. No, her plight, too, had stirred some chord in him that just kept on twanging. As a boy he had seen his father fight the kind of uneven contest in which Nora Wade was involved with Buck Cole. His father had, like Nora, refused to bow to his bigger neighbour's threats. One wintry day, it had cost him his life. And even now, many years on, the picture of his old man lying bleeding in the winter snows of Utah, with his mother's wails echoing across the bleak plain like an Irish banshee, was as vivid as it had been on that dark, brooding day.

He remembered the man who had stood over his father holding a smoking gun, too. He was a man not unlike Stryker Cole, full of anger and arrogance, his face flushed with a killer's lust. It was killing that man ten years later that had set him on the lonely trails he had since ridden, never settling in any one place too long, and always watching shadows.

Ben Dalton had done many jobs. He had driven cattle over the cow trails. Ridden shotgun for a stageline. Prospected for gold in the Yukon. Worn a star in a wide-open trail town. Even joined a troupe of travelling actors for a time, and spoken in that funny lingo which he did not understand a word of (penned by a fella called William Shakespeare) when the troupe played a circuit of city theatres back East. But, somehow, though he had tried and tried to give trouble a wide berth someone had always come on the prod, making it necessary for him to use his gun.

His father had always preached that a gun settled uneasily in a holster once it had been drawn that first time. Ben Dalton reckoned that there was a great dollop of truth in that theory. But he also believed that some men, of whom he was one, were destined in the wild and raw land they traversed to be called upon time and again to use a gun. And those were the men whose pride was unbending.

His father had had that kind of pride too, but he had also been a devout Quaker who hoped for the good he believed was in all men to shine through. He died believing that. And it was no help at all to the penniless woman and boy he left behind.

'We have to accept God's will, Ben,' his mother had said, once her anger and grief had subsided. 'We simply don't understand his plan for us.'

That was surely the truth, he had thought bitterly. At fifteen he had put on his first gun, and at eighteen he killed his first man; the man who had stood over his father with a smoking gun. By then the man had moved on from acting as a beef-baron's enforcer to gambling on the Mississippi.

'Why, son?' was the man's dying question to Ben Dalton.

He had replied, 'We simply don't understand God's plan for us, mister.'

The man who had killed his father died wearing exactly the same puzzled expression as his father had. The difference being that while his father had pondered on God's plan, his killer wondered why, after he'd done his will for so long, Satan had forsaken him.

Ben Dalton turned his horse, and headed back the way he had come.

Stryker Cole reached the darkest part of the trail well before Nora Wade. He lay in waiting for her arrival, his lust for her reaching ever higher peaks. A man driven by the most primitive of all desires, he was not thinking beyond the satiating of his needs.

Nora Wade drew rein at the start of the dark trail ahead. It was a part of the trail that had always unnerved her, and, for some reason, never more so than today. Most times she took an alternative but longer trail which passed through open, pleasant country. But now, anxious to be home, the longer trail did not appeal to her. Once the excitement of meeting Ben Dalton had died down, the scare of clashing with the Circle C bunch would upset Randy. She could not count on her husband to console and calm the boy. These days Ned Wade's temper was short, and his patience cobweb thin.

Setting her fears aside, Nora headed along the dark, wood-scented trail, quickening her pace as she reached the section where the intertwined tree-branches almost completely shut out the light. Here, in the gloomy silence, Nora's fears reached a feverish intensity.

Perched on the wooded slope overlooking the trail, Stryker Cole thought he had lost his prize when Nora hesitated and looked longingly back along the trail. His fever for her near stopped his heart. He slipped down through the trees, picking his steps carefully so as not to tread on a twig whose snap in the heavy stillness would alert Nora to his presence. When he reached an outcrop of rock directly over the narrowest part of the trail, he lay flat on his belly and waited, ready to pounce. The seconds ticked by. Each one seemed an hour long.

Nora Wade came up with all sorts of reasons for the chills running along her spine. Even now, well into the darkest section of the trail, she could turn back. However, her mind fixed on Randy's welfare, Nora fought down her inexplicable fears and rode on. When Stryker Cole sprang from cover and grabbed the reins of her horse, holding it fast, Nora saw in his contorted face all the reasons for her trepidation.

'Why, hello, Nora,' Stryker Cole crooned, his hand riding up under her skirts. She kicked out, but he easily danced aside. He leered. 'Now, Nora, I was counting on you being friendly, woman.'

'Get out of my way!' Nora railed.

She tried to take her horse on to its hindlegs to force Cole back. But he swiftly side-stepped the animal and pulled Nora from her saddle.

'Just a little kiss,' he said. Then, laughing harshly: 'To begin with . . . .'

Ben Dalton, who had taken a rougher hill-trail to close the gap between him and Nora Wade, came thundering out of the trees just as an enraged Stryker Cole was nursing his groin where Nora's knee had impacted. Ignoring his violated groin, the rancher's son swung about to deal with the new and deadly threat bearing down on him. He had his gun almost clear of leather when Dalton's boot caught him on the shoulder and spun him off his feet. Stryker Cole reeled backwards and crashed against a tree trunk. He was winded but still holding his gun when Dalton leaped from his horse. Stryker Cole's gun exploded. The breeze of the bullet fanned Ben Dalton's right cheek. He clawed for his own .45. Two more bullets chased him as he rolled away, spitting dirt in his face. Cole's gun was again drawing a bead on Ben Dalton when the gunfighter's Colt spat. Stryker Cole jerked, coughed, and blood seeped through his lips. A reflex action from dying nerve ends sent the bullet he had intended for Ben Dalton exploding into his own belly. But he felt no pain. He was already dead.

The fury over, Nora Wade clung to Ben Dalton, shivering at the narrow escape she had had. His consolation was brief. He put her at arm's length, and said stonily:

'You get on home, Nora.'

He went and draped Stryker Cole's body across his horse.

'Where are you headed, Ben?'

'The Circle C.'

'You can't do that,' Nora wailed. 'Buck Cole will kill you for sure.'

'I'll tell him what happened here—'

'And you think he'll believe you? You think

Buck Cole will want to admit that his only son was a rapist?'

'I can only place the facts before him, Nora. It's up to him to accept them or not.'

'And if he chooses to reject those facts, Ben?' Nora asked quietly.

'Then, Nora,' Ben Dalton sat wearily in his saddle, 'I guess I've got big trouble coming my way.'

CHAPTER SIX

Not long after Ben Dalton hit Circle C range, a rider broke free from a group of riders and rode helter-skelter ahead of Dalton to inform Buck Cole of the bad news coming his way. The rancher came from the house to meet Dalton at the gate leading into the ranch yard, his steps slowing to a sluggish crawl when he saw his son's body. Buck Cole's angry gaze settled on Ben Dalton.

'What happened? Your doing?'

'It is,' Dalton admitted, and added, 'But not from choice.' He went on to explain the circumstances of Stryker Cole's demise.

'You're a liar, Dalton!' the rancher railed. 'I'd never have claimed that my son was a saint – not much call for saints in these parts. But,' Buck Cole's face contorted with rage, 'he was no damn rapist!'

'You can ask Nora Wade,' Ben Dalton said calmly.

'Hah!' the rancher scoffed. His grey eyes narrowed. 'She in this with you?'

Arriving at a gallop, Blackjack Ryan leaped from his horse and took a stand alongside the Circle C boss.

'Let's be done with the talkin', Mr Cole. And let's get started with the necktie party for this bastard.'

Several more hands arrived at an equally brisk pace, expressing the same opinion. Several dangling ropes were on offer to Buck Cole. More men cut off Dalton's retreat. The gunfighter readied himself for action, but knew that if shooting started he was a dead man. Or if Buck Cole accepted the offer of a rope, he'd be equally dead.

'Would I be here if I'd murdered your son, Cole?' Dalton reasoned.

A glint of doubt flashed in the rancher's eyes, but vanished as quickly as it had flashed. 'If you were really smart, maybe that's exactly what you would do, Dalton,' Buck Cole opined.

'You fellas,' Dalton said, addressing the Circle C crew. 'You ever hear Stryker talk about Nora Wade in the way a man should not talk about a lady?'

Eyes met eyes. But it was left up to Blackjack Ryan to answer. He declared:

'Stryker wouldn't touch Nora Wade if she was the last woman in this whole darn county, mister.'

'I guess,' Dalton said, 'my question was a foolish one to expect an honest answer to.' Unflinching, he met Buck Cole's gaze. 'But Stryker did try to rape Nora Wade, Cole.'

Blackjack Ryan stormed forward. 'I say let's shut

his filthy mouth for good!'

Ben Dalton slid his Winchester from its saddle scabbard, and cautioned: 'I'll take at least six of you with me.'

Blackjack Ryan came up short as a bullet nipped his toecap. The men behind Ryan edged back.

'Sensible,' Dalton said.

Shaken by Dalton's action, Ryan said with false bravado, 'Your call, boss.'

Buck Cole said, 'Right now I'm not going to sacrifice any other man to your killer's lust, Dalton. But I'm warning you. You'll pay a full price for my son's death.'

'I see it differently, Cole,' Dalton replied stonily. 'I reckon your boy paid the full price for his actions.' He backed his horse out of the crowd, covering his would-be lynchers with the Winchester. 'Any man tries anything, the first bullet will be for your boss.'

He kept on backing off until he had opened up a goodly gap, then, turning, he rode off at a full gallop. Open, flat country stretched into the distance, with cover as sparse as hair on an egg. The Circle C crew dived for their guns. Bullets clipped the air around Dalton, riding full out and low in the saddle. When their guns failed to bring him down, and the gap grew wider, the Circle C rannies mounted up and gave hot pursuit, their guns still blasting.

Dalton's horse, though feisty in his response to the emergency, did not have a belly full of prime oats like the Circle C horses. Ben Dalton knew that the gap which was already closing would narrow all the more quickly in the next couple of minutes as his horse's legs and wind gave out. But maybe he wouldn't have that problem. Circle C bullets were getting nearer and more accurate all the time. It took great skill to bring down a fast moving target: a skill which, Dalton reckoned, with perhaps the exception of Blackjack Ryan, was not in the ranks of the Circle C rannies. But blasting as they were, volume would eventually tell.

A bullet nicked Dalton's shoulder, inflicting only a minor flesh wound. But even so, to a degree that might make all the difference, the graze would affect his control of the reins. Luckily it was his left shoulder, which would not impair his ability to use his gun when the time came. Sooner or later, when common sense took over from outrage, someone would tumble to the idea of aiming for the bigger target, his horse.

He could feel his mount's legs going. The gap between him and the Cole riders shortened by leaps and bounds. Dalton was also disadvantaged by his ignorance of the terrain. There were one or two promising-looking off-shoots, but their promise could peter out in a dead-end and leave him trapped at the mercy of his pursuers, who would show no mercy. Suddenly, another worrying twist materialized. Other Circle C riders, rounding up strays and alerted by the gunfire, angled Dalton's way, closing on him even faster than the main hunting party. This development left the gunfighter with no choice. He veered off, and hoped that the off-shoot he had taken would not be his undoing.

The sudden switch in direction took the last of his horse's strength. The beast stumbled. The ground swept up to meet Dalton. He fought his headlong lunge. The bite of a rope round his shoulders yanked him from the saddle. Ben Dalton fell heavily, and lay winded.

The main bunch of Circle C riders came up fast.

Blackjack Ryan complimented the rope thrower.

'Nice ropin', Hal. Now slide that rope round his neck, and get him to a tree.' A duo of beefy rannies hauled Ben Dalton to his feet. Ryan pointed to a lofty oak. 'Hanged my first man from that tree.'

Uneasy with the drastic action proposed, one of Hal's partners asked: 'Just what did this *hombre* do, Blackjack?'

'Gunned down Stryker Cole in cold blood, Deke.'

'That a fact,' Deke growled, eyeing Ben Dalton with scathing contempt. 'Guess hangin's 'bout right for him then.'

'We're wastin' time. String him up, Hal,' Ryan ordered.

'The tale's a lot curlier than Ryan says,' Ben Dalton told Deke. 'Stryker Cole tried to rape Nora Wade.'

'Rape?' Deke spat in disgust. He pondered.

'Come to think of it, Stryker did have a' awful yen for Nora Wade, fellas.'

Blackjack Ryan raked Dalton's left cheek with his gun butt. 'You talk too much, Dalton.' Turning to Deke, he growled: 'You draw Cole dollars. You do Cole biddin'.'

Ryan's stance shifted threateningly.

'You with us or agin us, Deke?'

The blood drained from Deke's face. 'With ya, o' course, Blackjack,' he yelped.

'Then,' Ryan handed the lynch rope to Deke, 'I guess the honour's all yours.'

Deke gulped. 'I ain't never hanged no one, Blackjack.'

'There's always a first time,' Ryan snarled.

'This is murder, plain and simple,' Ben Dalton told Deke. 'Do you want that kind of stain on your soul when you meet your Maker?'

Blackjack Ryan again threatened Dalton with his gun butt.

'Shut your mouth!'

'I ain't scared none,' Deke declared. But the quiver in his voice said otherwise. 'Get him in the saddle, fellas.'

Dalton mounted, Deke raised his hand to slap the horse's haunches. 'Yeeeehaaaa!'

CHAPTER SEVEN

Ben Dalton closed his eyes and waited for his horse to bolt. He tensed himself, uselessly so, for the tightening of the rope would be relentless, and there would be no fighting it. But what sound had he heard? Just before Deke cried out. The crack of a rifle? Whose rifle? He opened his eyes to see Deke topple backwards. The rifle spoke again from a nearby pine-clad knoll, its wisp of smoke curling up like a arthritic finger accusing heaven. The horse under Dalton, excited by the gunfire and scattering of men, bolted. Dalton reached up and grabbed the rope above the noose and hauled himself up just as he sat on air. His arms were almost wrenched from their sockets, and the excruciating pain took his breath away. He felt his hands slide down the rope. He could only hold on for seconds. His escape from the lynching was cruel. Because all it had done was give him thirty seconds of false hope.

But lady luck again changed her mind. The shooter's next bullet split the lynch rope and Ben

Dalton crashed to the ground. Blackjack Ryan sprang from behind a boulder at the edge of the trail, six-gun cocked to menace Dalton. The .45 was spun out of his grasp by the deadly accurate rifle-toter. On the knoll, Nora Wade stepped from cover, Winchester squarely on Ryan.

'Mount up and ride,' she ordered the Circle C crew.

Ryan said, 'You've just heaped problems on problems for yourself, ma'am. Buck Cole ain't—'

Nora Wade rattled back: 'I've long since stopped worrying about Buck Cole's likes and dislikes, Ryan. You tell your boss that it was as Ben Dalton said.'

Ryan snorted. 'Mr Cole ain't nohow goin' to believe that yarn.'

'I guess it'll be hard medicine to swallow at that. No man wants to admit that his son is a rapist.'

Nora's gaze swept the Circle C hands. 'But you men know how Stryker Cole talked in the bunkhouse and saloon. And if there's one decent man among you, you'll tell Buck Cole about it.'

The riders exchanged guilty glances and hung their heads low.

'You're no better than the snakes who crawl on their bellies,' Nora blasted them. 'Get out of my sight before I'm tempted to use this rifle again!'

With glowering faces, the men turned their horses in the direction of the Circle C. Before departing, Blackjack Ryan promised Ben Dalton:

'That noose is still danglin', Dalton.'

'Take my advice,' the gunfighter said. 'Give me a wide berth in future, if you want to stay above ground, mister.'

Ryan spat. 'You won't always have a skirt to hide behind, Dalton.'

The riders thundered out of the leafy glade. Quickly, Nora Wade reached higher ground to monitor their departure.

'That bend in the trail up ahead,' she explained. 'Might just be a temptation for them to double back.'

Her move was a wise one. The riders, on Ryan's say-so, swung about. Nora's timely volley changed their minds again.

'Keep right on going, Ryan,' Nora called out. 'All the way to the Circle C bunkhouse.'

Fuming, Blackjack Ryan galloped off. Nora began to shake.

'Close call,' she said.

Ben Dalton took her in his arms until the shudders passed – twenty seconds, maybe. But it was twenty seconds too long. He liked the feeling of Nora Wade in his arms way too much.

'Pretty fancy shooting, Nora,' he complimented, when she relaxed. 'Where did you learn to handle a rifle like that?'

'My Uncle John taught me. He became my guardian when my folks died of fever. He was a marshal in a wide-open border town. He figured that living with him brought dangers that needed my being able to shoot quick and shoot straight.'

'He was an ace tutor,' Dalton opined.

'But I never liked the feel of a gun, Ben. For me it was like handling a wriggling snake.'

'It's a good feeling, Nora,' Dalton assured her. 'It means that you'll only pick one up when it's absolutely necessary.' He grinned. 'But I'm sure glad that your Uncle John taught you to shoot.'

The day had clouded over, its early promise snuffed out under thunderheads rolling up from the south, and the mood of the countryside had changed too. The range did not look as green as it had looked, and the mountains to the east of the valley were black and scowling.

'It'll rain soon,' Nora said.

'Looks that way,' Dalton agreed.

'You'd best make tracks, Ben. While you still can.'

'I ain't leaving with a cloud hanging over me, Nora. I'll head for town. Explain to the sheriff what happened. Don't want the law dogging my tail for a murder I didn't commit.'

Nora was shaking her head as if she had found the fool of all fools.

'Talking to Eli Bracken isn't going to do one whit of good, Ben.'

'Eli Bracken?' Dalton questioned, eyes brimming with interest. The surprise in Ben Dalton's voice had Nora glancing his way.

'Tall?' Dalton asked.

Nora nodded.

'Vulture's eyes?'

Nora nodded again.

'Doesn't know what soap is, and as crooked as a rattler's slide?'

Nora nodded for a third time, and said, 'You know Eli Bracken, sure enough.'

'He's the law hereabouts?'

Nora sighed wearily. 'He is.'

'In Buck Cole's pocket, too, I figure.'

'He was Stryker's fixer. But Eli Bracken isn't particular about who fills his pocket.' Nora Wade's curiosity piqued, she asked, 'Where did you cross paths with him, Ben?'

'Not with Eli. With his twin.'

'His twin!' Nora exclaimed. 'You mean that there's two of those ugly gazaboos around?'

'Just one, now. Eli. I killed his brother Nate.'

'Ki . . . ?' Nora Wade's shoulders slumped. 'I guess you're going to be as welcome in Hawk's Bend as a saint in hell, Ben Dalton.'

'I expect I will, Nora,' the gunfighter drawled lazily.

Nora Wade's advice was: 'Skip town. Head straight for the border.'

Ben Dalton looked about the countryside.

'You know, Nora, this country kind of grows on a man. I was thinking about putting down roots here.'

Nora's heart took a funny little leap, the reason for which she was not sure of. Or was she? But it felt good. It hadn't leaped that way for a long time. There was no time to think about the butterflies

65

fluttering in her tummy. It wouldn't matter anyway. Ben Dalton could not remain in Hawk's Bend. Not if he wanted to stay alive.

The gunfighter's eyes were dreamy.

'A man grows weary of the trail, Nora. Gets really tired of only having his horse to talk to of an evening. And pretty soon my bones will begin to ache . . . .'

Nora laughed. 'That's a long way off, Ben.'

Dalton's gaze was soulful.

'Is it, Nora? Time races, while a man gets slower. Every turn of the trail nowdays seems to bring another youngster bucking to beat Ben Dalton to the draw. Earn himself a reputation. Soon, I reckon, one of those kids will, too.'

'They say that you're the fastest?' Nora said.

'Yeah. That's the curse I have to live with.'

Nora hoped she did not sound too critical when she said: 'You didn't have to become a gunfighter, Ben.'

Dalton considered her point. Thinking back to the anger in him at the man who had murdered his father, he concluded:

'Yes, Nora. I had to. But the thing with killing is it's voracious appetite. The second I killed the man who murdered my pa, I knew that from then on killing would stalk me. But,' he sighed wearily, 'a man gets to hope that there's someplace where he can hang up his gun for good. I thought . . .'

His voice drifted away.

Ben Dalton's lonely tone tugged at Nora Wade's

heart. She watched the hope which had welled up in his eyes vanish like autumn smoke on a breeze. She was tempted to change her mind and urge him to remain in Hawk's Bend. Part of her reason for doing so was selfish and likely sinful, too. And part of her reason was to reignite the hope in Ben Dalton's eyes. But, hard as it was, Nora curbed her urge, knowing that if he stayed on in Hawk's Bend the odds against his survival were too great to ponder on or risk.

'There'll be other towns, other places, Ben,' Nora said quietly, keeping her voice hushed to cover the cracks in it.

Ben Dalton's cheeriness was false.

'Sure there will, Nora. Lots of towns.'

Secretly, Ben Dalton had been longing for Nora Wade to change her mind and persuade him to stay. But he also understood her reasons for wanting him to leave. That sharp intake of breath when she was in his arms was one. Another was the trouble that his hanging around would bring on her head. With him gone, the blame for Stryker Cole's death could be placed squarely on him. In time, Nora and Buck Cole would strike a deal on the creek. The Circle C would expand. Some lawman somewhere would be chasing him for Stryker Cole's murder. Buck Cole's grief would lessen, and Nora Wade might sometimes think of him, but perhaps not very often. Maybe when a dodger with his face on it turned up. Or when someone spoke his name. And sooner or later, probably sooner, word would come of Ben Dalton's death on a lonely trail or dogs-ear town. Depressingly, Ben Dalton reckoned that that was the way things were ordained from the second that that man gunned down his father, and he went seeking revenge.

'Goodbye, Nora,' he said. 'Hope things work out between you and Buck Cole.'

He swung his horse and rode out of the glade, not looking back. Tears washed Nora Wade's eyes. She had heard good and bad about Ben Dalton. But having known the man, even for the brief time she had, Nora now discounted the bad. Ben Dalton stood head and shoulders above other men, and she regretted his departure keenly in the deepest recesses of her heart.

Dalton let his tired horse wander, letting it find its own trail. He had picked them up to now and none had been much good. Maybe horse-sense would set him on a better trail? He put Nora Wade firmly from his mind. He knew that thinking about her in the lonely hours ahead would be the way to madness. He supposed that in the back of his mind, if he were totally honest, his desire to stay in Hawk's Bend was tied in to some as yet undefined scheme, that would bring him and Nora together. But it was a plan whose roots were in shallow ground. Nora Wade was another man's woman, and he had no right to her whatsoever.

His logical thinking did nothing to still Ben Dalton's longing.

CHAPTER EIGHT

Sheriff Eli Bracken had just lit up a Mexican cheroot he had a fondness for, and was exhaling its foul smoke when the law office door opened.

'Wha'd'ya want?' he growled at the bald head that poked in.

'A word, Sheriff Bracken.'

Seconds later, Eli Bracken sprang out of his chair at the news the whiskey drummer had brought to town.

'You sure?' Bracken snarled.

'Seen him face to face a coupla times in my travels,' the whiskey drummer assured the Hawk's Bend sheriff. 'As close as we are right now, Sheriff.' The pint-sized drummer slyly asked: 'Didn't Ben Dalton kill your brother, Sheriff Bracken?'

The drummer's question was mischievous. He had been right there when Dalton had killed Nate Bracken. That was one of the times he had been face to face with Ben Dalton, having collided with him at the batwings of a saloon, just before he stepped in to the street on Nate Bracken's call.

Bracken swept the diminutive whiskey-drummer aside as he strode to the law office door. He yanked open the door and hollered along the street to where his deputy was lounging outside the saloon talking to one of the doves:

'Charlie . . . Now!' he added, as the deputy, used to Bracken's tantrums, was sluggish in his response. When Charlie Delap reached the law office, running, the sheriff threw a fistful of deputies stars across the desk. 'Round up a posse. Fast.'

Being unaware of recent developments, the deputy ill-advisedly prevaricated.

'Posse, Eli?'

'You deaf as well as stupid!' Bracken ranted, his muddy eyes blazing to life with anger.

'No, sir.'

'Then do as I say.'

'Yes, Sheriff.'

Delap scooped up the deputies' emblems and hurried from the office.

'Dalton will be long gone by now, Sheriff,' the whiskey drummer said. 'It's more than two hours since I seen him talking to a woman at Bowie Creek.'

Eli Bracken's eyebrows arched. 'A woman, you say? Bowie Creek, huh? A real looker?'

'My, oh my, yes,' the drummer enthused.

'Long dark hair? Hazel eyes that could stir a man to near insanity?'

'Dark hair, yes,' the drummer confirmed. He

giggled. 'Didn't get close enough to look into her eyes, Sheriff. No way I was going into that creek, with Ben Dalton 'round.'

'Hear what they were talking about?' Bracken questioned closely.

'Sheriff,' the drummer protested righteously.

'Ya did, for sure,' the Hawk's Bend lawman growled.

The whiskey drummer maintained his righteous rebuttal. 'Really, Sheriff . . .'

Eli Bracken grabbed a fistful of the drummer's shirt. 'What did ya hear? Spit it out. Or get ready to spit out your teeth.'

The drummer gulped. 'They were talking about some fella by the name of Buck Cole.'

'Figgers,' Bracken growled. 'Go on.'

'Well, the woman was trying to enlist Ben Dalton's help. Seems this woman is having trouble with this fella, Cole.'

Eli Bracken laughed, a surprisingly humorous laugh for the scowling man he was. 'And you heard all this just in passing, eh, drummer?' He cruelly teased the shaking man. 'Maybe, when I meet up with Dalton, I'll tell him about how you cocked an ear to hear his business.'

The whiskey drummer paled. 'You wouldn't, Sheriff?'

'Depends on how long I'm in the saddle hunting Dalton down. Now get outa here.'

The snivelling whiskey drummer scampered from the law office. Bracken's twisted sense of humour was tickled on seeing the drummer scurry directly to the livery for his horse.

'Keep that pace up, drummer,' the sheriff chuckled. 'And you'll be selling tequila instead of whiskey.'

Charlie Delap had assembled a rag-bag assortment of drunks and layabouts in front of the saloon. Bracken stormed along the boardwalk, hauled four men out of their saddles and shoved them back inside the saloon.

'I want men I won't have to stop every couple of minutes to pick up, Charlie,' he berated his deputy. His hostile glare travelled over the excuse for a posse, a couple of whom were tilting sideways in their saddles, but would probably straighten once they got going.

'These men are all I can get, Sheriff,' Delap moaned.

'It ain't easy to get fellas to step on Ben Dalton's tail, Eli,' the most senior and least drunk of the rag-tag posse declared. He licked dry lips. 'Only a certain kinda desperate man would be loco enough to want to try.'

Bracken recognized the truth of the man's words. But there was also another truth, and that was that Eli Bracken was a man with little respect in town. It was no secret that he took every opportunity presented to him to line his pockets. So the law in Hawk's Bend always favoured those who could buy it. No one ever said anything. Outspokenness was too dangerous an indulgence.

Those who had in the past spoken out had paid a high price for their opposition to Bracken and his cronies. The opinion in Hawk's Bend, though only expressed in closed circles where a man could trust his listeners, was that no law would be preferable to Bracken law. So when a posse was needed the only applicants for the job (though most family men in town could do with the twenty dollars fee paid for the duty) were those whose need was desperate in the extreme – like a hell-fire thirst.

'Ben Dalton's done nothing wrong in these parts, Sheriff,' Abe Benjamin, the hardware-store owner, a fair-minded man, reminded Bracken, having learned from the fleeing drummer the purpose of the posse. 'The cost of this posse will have to be met out of town funds.' His eyes did a quick count. 'If there's that much in the town coffers to begin with.'

'Dalton's a killer,' Bracken growled.

Abe Benjamin persisted in his opposition.

'The way I heard it was that since Ben Dalton avenged his father's murder, he's had to protect himself from every tinhorn gunnie he crossed paths with. More sinned against than sinning. And,' he emphasized, 'if it's snakes in the grass you're after, well, there's more than enough around here to begin with.'

'Draw in your horns, Abe,' a friend standing alongside the hardware-store owner advised in an undertone. 'You're locking horns with the devil.'

However, Abe Benjamin continued with his

opposition to the posse which he knew, as every man did, was being rounded up to serve Eli Bracken's own ends.

'I figure, Sheriff,' Benjamin said, 'that unless you show good cause for hunting down Ben Dalton, the cost of this posse should come out of your own pocket.'

'My pocket?' Bracken yelped.

'For God's sake, Abe,' his friend murmured. 'Let it go.'

But, grim-faced, Benjamin pressed: 'That's the way I see it, Sheriff. As administrator of this town's funds, I'm refusing to sanction this posse.'

He addressed the mounted men.

'Not a nickel, gents.'

The men's eyes flashed Eli Bracken's way. One man asked:

'You willin' to cough up, Eli?'

Bracken shifted uneasily. 'Maybe . . . five dollars a man,' he grumbled.

'Five dollars a man?' another man yelped, already out of his saddle. He headed back into the saloon. 'I ain't riskin' my hide goin' up agin Ben Dalton for no five dollars.'

The remainder of the men were also dismounting.

Benjamin said triumphantly, 'I guess that's the end of the posse, Sheriff Bracken.'

The men around the hardware-store owner gained courage from Benjamin's spirited stance, the first by any man in a long time. It started what at first was a mumbled endorsement of Benjamin's stand, but it soon took hold and became a full-blown backing.

Eli Bracken's stonily evil gaze settled on Abe Benjamin. He declared: 'Benjamin, I reckon you're interfering with the administration of justice. Town law forty-one says that that's a jailing offence, mister.'

Encouraged by his initial victory over Eli Bracken and the support his stand had received, Abe Benjamin did not back down.

'You have brought nothing but shame on an honourable badge, Bracken,' he said. 'And in my book you have long since forfeited all right to wear it.'

'That a fact, Benjamin,' Bracken said, his eyes darting over the crowd to gauge the backing for the storekeeper's renewed and even more dangerous attack on him. He threatened: 'Any man who backs Benjamin's interference is guilty of the same offence!'

His threat fell on deaf ears.

Bracken saw that he had the makings of a rebellion on his hands. His eyes shifted to a man who had, in the past, partnered him in various nefarious acts. The man read perfectly the message in Bracken's eyes. He edged right up alongside Abe Benjamin and nudged his elbow. The hardware-store owner's hand jerked.

'He's goin' for a gun, Sheriff,' the man yelled.

Eli Bracken took his cue. He drew his six-gun

and sent a bullet winging dead centre of Abe Benjamin's chest, blasting the store-owner clear off his feet. The crowd scattered in confusion and panic, giving Bracken's crony the chance to kneel alongside Benjamin under the guise of going to his aid. He slipped his pistol into Benjamin's hand. The transfer of the gun was snake-oil slick. Then he hared off to get the town doctor. But his real purpose was to slip away in the confusion. Someone might get curious about his empty holster.

There were doubters, of course. But with the storekeeper holding a six-gun, everyone knew that in a court of law Bracken would be vindicated as having acted in self-defence. The confusion was quickly added to by the thunderous arrival of a Circle C rider, yelling:

'Stryker Cole's been murdered by Ben Dalton, Sheriff!'

CHAPTER NINE

'Where the hell've you been, woman?' Ned Wade angrily challenged his wife. 'This boy's,' he dragged Randy Wade roughly from the cabin and flung him towards Nora as she dismounted, 'been actin' more loco than ever!'

Nora grabbed Randy as he stumbled towards her and she held him tenderly. She saw that his face was tear-stained, and his eyes bloodshot from crying. She glared at her husband with open contempt.

'It's OK honey,' Nora consoled the whimpering boy. 'I'm home now.'

'Where've you been?' Wade demanded again.

Enraged by her husband's treatment of their simple-minded son, Nora blurted out: 'I've been with Ben Dalton!'

The way Nora couched her words left no doubt as to how she would have wanted that meeting to have panned out.

'Come back inside the house now, Randy,' Nora said.

Randy cowered. 'No, Ma.'

Ned Wade sprang from the porch, unstrapping his belt. 'You get inside the house right now, boy,' he barked. 'Or so help me I'll take the skin off your back.'

Nora Wade blocked her husband's charge.

'You lay a finger on him,' she warned Ned Wade. 'And I'll kill you, so help me God!'

Dismissive of Nora's threat, he lunged past her, shoving her to one side. Nora grabbed the rifle from her saddle scabbard. Wade's steps faltered on hearing a bullet slot into the rifle's breech. He turned slowly, his face livid with fury.

'You'd hold a rifle on your own husband,' he snarled.

'Not only hold it, Ned,' Nora said. 'Use it too, if needs be.'

The confrontation between his parents heaped confusion on confusion for Randy Wade. Unable to bring reason to bear, he ran away.

'Randy,' Nora called, desperately. 'Come back.'

'Let him go,' Ned Wade growled. 'We'll be rid of the shame.'

Nora Wade's finger curled around the rifle's trigger. The devil prodded her to pull it. Fighting her temptation, she flung the rifle aside and ran after Randy.

'Crazy woman, crazy boy, I guess,' Wade snorted.

Ben Dalton, still pondering on how life sometimes offers a chance only to grab it back cruelly again, drew rein in a gully that had a trickling stream, good cover, and grass for his horse. He sat with his back against a boulder, took the makings from his vest pocket, and rolled a smoke. He was not a regular puffer of the weed, but at times when the world weighed heavy on his shoulders he liked to think with a smoke going.

It was late in the day, and he reckoned that he might as well bed down for the night. There was a chill wind coming up and the gully offered reasonable shelter from its bite. He was a man used to sleeping under the stars, but, of late, with the years piling on, he had begun to hanker for a roof and a feather bed. He was only thirty-five, but already he had the morning pangs of stiffening joints. The fact was that, no matter how a man protected himself from the elements, sleeping in creeks and draws and in draughty barns took its toll. And of late, Dalton had found himself looking at each new town as a place to hang up his gun, find honest work, and a good woman to settle down with. Up to now he had drawn a blank. But for a while, today, he had hoped that his search had ended.

'Well, it damn well hasn't!' he growled. 'And you'd best head out of this neck o' the woods pronto, if you don't want to be strung up.'

He had watched for sign, frequently checking his back trail. It surprised him that there had been none. He was at a loss as to why there hadn't been.

Despite his best efforts to ignore Nora Wade,

she crept into his thoughts. He worried that she would suffer Buck Cole's backlash. A couple of times he had thought about turning back, but maybe his presence would only bring more grief on the Wades. He'd sleep on the problem. Come morning he would see things more clearly, he hoped. With night fast closing in there was little he could do anyway. Or was there? Darkness would give him the cover to make his way back with relative safety to the Wade homestead. Ben Dalton had faced many dilemmas in his time, but he had never faced a situation which had him in the kind of lather he was now in. Normally, he was not a man who dithered. However, he was fast discovering that since he had met Nora Wade, he was not the man he had previously been. That made him angry. And in a strange way, pleased, too.

When the Circle C crew arrived back at the ranch without Ben Dalton in tow or draped across his saddle, Buck Cole's rage was white-hot.

'He put the run under all of you?' he ranted.

'No,' Blackjack Ryan said, sheepishly. 'We had a rope slung when—'

'When what?'

Ryan mumbled: 'Nora Wade turned up.'

'Nora Wade,' the rancher yelled. 'A skirt put the run on you lot?'

'She had us cold, boss,' one of the men said.

'Yeah,' another put in admiringly. 'She can use a darn rifle better than any man I've ever known.'

'Get out of my sight!' the rancher bellowed. 'And be off Cole range before I can saddle up and come after you.'

'We ain't got paid this month, Mr Cole,' Ryan whinged.

'You got grub, and you've got the horses you're sitting on.' He grabbed a rifle resting against a corral post and cocked it. 'And you'll get lead in the gut if you don't get out of my sight!'

One of the crew, riled, said, 'I ain't budgin' without my money.'

Buck Cole's rifle cracked. The man clutched at his right arm. Cole warned, 'The next slug will be dead centre of your heart, Kowski.'

Blackjack Ryan and another man named Clay Ambrose, a crony of Ryan's, hung back. Buck Cole swung the rifle their way.

'I got an idea that might be worth listenin' to, Mr Cole,' Ryan said, nervously licking dry lips.

'An idea? What kind of idea?'

'A coupla men instead of a small army would best be suited to snaring Dalton, I figure.'

'Go on.'

More at ease, Ryan elaborated. 'A posse or Circle C outfit would make noise, send up lots of dust. I reckon that me and Clay could get close enough to Dalton to spit in his eye before he knew we were there.'

'Maybe,' Cole conceded.

Ryan let his hand rest casually on his right hip, but ready to dive lower to his gun should Buck

Cole take umbrage at what came next.

'You know, I've been thinkin' for a spell 'bout movin' on . . .'

It was true that he had been thinking about moving on, but not for a spell as he had stated. His desire to quit Circle C range had only come to the fore with Stryker Cole's demise. Without his patronage, honest labour faced him, and he was a man with a keen aversion to hard work. New pastures beckoned. But with empty pockets life would be hard.

So:

'Thing is, Mr Cole. A man can't live on good intentions and fresh air. If you catch my drift?'

'I catch it good, Ryan,' Cole grumbled. 'How much?'

Now came the most difficult part of the negotiations. Too much, and Cole would probably whip the skin off his back. Too little, and a golden chance to feather his nest would be gone.

'How much?' Cole pressed.

'A thou – thousand dollars apiece?' Ryan stammered.

It came as a complete surprise to Ryan when Cole readily agreed.

'It's a deal. But not a nickel until you deliver Ben Dalton. Dead or alive. Don't much care one way or the other.' He called an old-timer who odd-jobbed around the ranch to him. 'Head to town, Bony. Tell Eli Bracken that plans are in hand to snare Dalton.'

He turned and strode towards the house.

'Not a damn nickel, Blackjack,' Ambrose griped. 'I say we should let Buck Cole go to hell!'

It was a sentiment Ryan fully shared. But he also knew that to try and corral Buck Cole in the ugly mood he was in, might be more dangerous than kissing a rattler. He told Ambrose:

'We can wait a while longer to hit the trail rich, Clay.'

Clay Ambrose snorted. 'A thousand dollars ain't rich, Blackjack.'

No. But two thousand dollars wasn't bad. Because that's what Ryan intended having as soon as Ambrose showed him his back after collecting Dalton's bounty.

CHAPTER TEN

Ben Dalton came awake, but remained perfectly still. He had heard something. Maybe a nocturnal creature on the prowl. Maybe, too, it had two legs instead of four.

He waited.

Nothing.

He stirred, giving the impression that he had been disturbed, but had not woken. Under the blankets his finger was curled round the trigger of a cocked pistol. Sleeping perfectly still, which was a necessary requirement for sleeping with a cocked six-gun, was a skill which an old Cheyenne had taught him, as a compensation for nursing the old man through a winter fever. Over the years, the Cheyenne's lesson had saved his life more than once.

There it was again – the merest rustle of grass.

Dalton tensed.

Crouched between twin boulders, Blackjack Ryan and Clay Ambrose watched the peaceful scene in the moon-dappled gully.

'Out cold, looks like,' Ambrose whispered.

'Looks that way,' Ryan agreed.

'Kinda nice o' Dalton to leave his gunbelt hangin' on his saddle horn, ain't it?' was Ambrose's opinion.

Ben Dalton hoped that his caller, or callers, did not spot that the holster was the wrong way round to hide the fact that it was empty.

'Rifle in its scabbard, too,' Ryan murmured, a mite uneasily.

'What're you frettin' bout, Blackjack?'

'Didn't figger on Dalton bein' no fool, that's all.'

Clay Ambrose was dismissive of Blackjack Ryan's caution.

'Escapin' a noose makes a man tired and ready for sleep.'

'Careless, too?' Ryan pondered.

'Look,' Ambrose said, struggling to keep a rein on his impatience, 'his guns, for whatever reason, are on full view. That means they ain't with him. He's asleep. So let's just plug him, fling him over his saddle, and collect that damn bounty.'

Ambrose blew on his fingers, his eyes glowing greedily.

'I can't wait to get the feel of Buck Cole's dollars, Blackjack.'

Ryan, though not fully at ease, agreed.

'Let's do it.'

Ben Dalton had feared for a moment that Blackjack Ryan's caution would work against him, and that he would simply shoot from where he was.

But now it looked like the old Cheyenne's ruse was about to save his hide once more.

Nora Wade tossed restlessly. She had woken suddenly with Ben Dalton on her mind, troubled, and her apprehension would not go away. In fact it increased in intensity until it clamped her heart. Ned Wade, fearful of Cole reprisals, had kept watch. Their earlier argument had become a sullen, wordless impasse that grieved Nora. As always, Ned's remorse was great, but the rift between him and Randy, who could not understand as Nora did, grew wider and more fraught every day. For herself, remembering how good a man Ned Wade had been, she could take his tantrums. But she could not accept his grudging ways towards Randy. It was not his fault that he had been born the way he had. That flaw lay in her or Ned, or a combination of both. Unable to rest, Nora got up and went to the main room of the cabin where her husband was sitting at a window keeping watch. The fire had almost died and it was cold.

'You'll catch your death, Nora,' Ned Wade said softly. 'Best you stay in bed.'

'I'll take my turn, Ned,' she said. 'A chill will do you more harm than it will me.'

'Don't matter much,' he said, his gaze far off. 'You and the boy (he had never called him Randy since his mental incapacitation had become obvious) would be better off without me, Nora.'

87

'Don't talk foolish, Ned,' she gently chided him.

'It's the truth, Nora. And you know it is,' he stately bluntly.

Unable to meet her husband's eyes, Nora stoked the fire and added a couple of logs to it. Chore completed, she said, 'I'll make fresh coffee.'

'Nora . . .'

'Yes, Ned.'

'This fella Dalton. Did he . . . Well, make an impression on you?'

'An impression?' Nora hedged.

'You know what I mean, Nora.'

Her answer, after due consideration, was an honest one. 'I'm not sure, Ned. Maybe he did. Maybe he didn't.'

'You'll be a widder soon, Nora . . .'

'Don't talk so, Ned.'

'It's a fact,' he said impatiently. 'No use in denying it any more.' Troubled, he continued: 'When I'm gone you'll be a woman alone. This country is no place for a woman to be on her own.' His eyes filled. 'And there's Randy. I haven't been fair to that boy, not by a long shot.'

Nora Wade's heart went out to her husband. She had never before seen hurt and regret in his eyes as she was witnessing it now. The good man that was once Ned Wade was back. If she could ever again love him, it was in that moment.

Wade went on:

'He'll need fathering too, Nora.'

'What are you trying to say, Ned?' Nora asked

softly, a lump in her throat.

'I'm saying that when I'm no longer around, Ben Dalton, if he was willing to hang up his gun, might make you a fine husband and Randy a good father.'

'Are you telling me—'

'No, dammit! I'm talking about when I'm gone. And I'll ask you to give me your word this very second that while I'm still around you won't give yourself to Ben Dalton, Nora.'

She took his hands in hers. 'I promise, Ned.'

'That's good enough for me. Now where the hell is that coffee you were brewing?'

Ben Dalton opened one eye. The ambushers, for he was certain now that that was what they were, were as yet shadows among shadows. But there was something familar about the leading man's gait. Blackjack Ryan! Now Buck Cole's strategy became clear, and explained the lack of earlier pursuit. Instead of a bunch of riders, stirring up a mile-wide dust cloud, the rancher had cleverly opted for stealth by sending only two men to settle accounts.

Ryan paused at midpoint, his eyes warily watching Dalton's blanket-covered bulk for any hint of movement. Impatient with what he saw as Ryan's namby-pambiness, Clay Ambrose groused.

'Let's get it done with, Blackjack.' His eyes darted about. 'This gully ain't none to my liking.'

Ryan drew his six-gun and went forward again.

They had their thumbs on the hammers when:

'Howdy, gents.'

Ben Dalton flung his blanket aside, six-gun blazing. Ambrose grabbed his gut, grunted, and toppled forward. Blackjack Ryan reacted swiftly, blasting at Dalton, but the gunfighter had already ducked. The bullet buzzed off a tree to Dalton's right. However, the evasive action forced on him gave Ryan time to vanish into the darkness. Seconds later the thunder of hoofs disturbed the night. Dalton cut loose with a couple of rounds in Ryan's general direction to no avail.

'I'll come looking, Ryan,' Dalton called out. 'That you can bet on, mister.'

With all hope of sleep gone, Ben Dalton rolled another smoke. Come morning, he decided, he was heading back to Hawk's Bend to finish unfinished business.

CHAPTER ELEVEN

Eli Bracken took the valise which he kept at the ready in every town he had milked from under the bedroom floorboards of the clapboard house that went with the sheriff's job. He checked its contents to the cent. Satisfied, he then went into two more rooms and prised up floorboards in those rooms also. He counted the bundles of ill-gotten dollars, quite an amount of which had been contributed by Stryker Cole for nefarious deeds done, and returned to the bedroom where he stuffed them into a second valise. In all, there was $10,000, the booty for murder and mayhem. Hidden in a tin box in a hidy-hole outside of town were the proceeds from a bank robbery he had performed in the previous town he was in, after which he had railroaded two men to the gallows via shotgun justice to cover his tracks. All in all, he had the best part of $20,000.

He counselled himself not to be greedy and hightail it out of Hawk's Bend before the town turned on him. That would not have happened when Stryker Cole was around. But Buck Cole had always been cool towards him, making no secret of his disapproval of Stryker's friendship with him. There would be no support from that quarter, should trouble come calling. Shooting Abe Benjamin had stirred strong feelings among the decent folk of Hawk's Bend. As yet, no one had got up enough steam to sling a rope for him. But sooner rather than later, he reckoned, someone would.

He knew the wise thing to do would be to high-tail it right then and there. But there was a shipment of money coming into the bank in a couple of days, and it would be mighty pleasing to add that to the pile he already had. If he succeeded in doing that, he'd never again see a poor day. He could go wherever he had a hankering to go. Maybe South America, where such a poke would virtually make him a king. He'd have to think about it. Maybe he should take the risk to reap the rewards.

Ben Dalton had made tracks. He'd have liked to hang him for killing his brother Nate. However, Buck Cole had sent word to shelve the posse, and bucking the rancher would be an entirely different proposition to bucking a storekeeper. Cole would likely hang, draw and quarter him if he interfered with his business. And if Nate had been stupid enough to call Ben Dalton out in the first place, he deserved what he got. Anyway, he could always hire a fast gun to go after Dalton. Murder by proxy was safer, when it entailed going up against a gun-slick *hombre* like Ben Dalton.

There was, too, another opportunity to enrich himself – blackmailing Buck Cole. Stryker was dead. But, he figured, Cole senior would pay good dollars to keep news of the dark side of his son's nature secret.

And there were the Wades, he thought bitterly – particularly Nora Wade. She, he held responsible for the end of a sweet deal with Stryker Cole. And for that she would have to pay a price. He already had Nora Wade's punishment planned.

Deciding to squeeze Buck Cole and take his revenge on the Wades, Bracken left the house, checking first that the streets were quiet and his passage would go unnoticed. He walked his horse to the edge of town to avoid stirring curiosity. The night had started out with a full moon on show, but cloud had brought a cold rain and a strong wind – not the kind of night in which a man would freely choose to be out and about.

He passed unnoticed. His first port of call would be the Circle C. Then he would round up a couple of trusted hardcases and swing by the Wade homestead to extract that price which he had in mind.

CHAPTER TWELVE

'What do you want, Bracken?' Buck Cole spat sourly.

'Sorry to hear about Stryker, Mr Cole,' Bracken commiserated, not caring a fig for the rancher's suffering or Stryker Cole's fate.

'State your business and be gone!' the rancher stated bluntly. 'I've never liked you, Bracken. And I never wanted Stryker to have anything to do with you. I'd have preferred my boy to be friends with a rattler sooner than you.

'Sticks and stones,' the sheriff chuckled, and then snarled: 'I think it's time you learned some truths about Stryker.'

'Truths?'

The Hawk's Bend sheriff gave a litany of the services he had rendered to the rancher's son. Acts of plunder, terrorism and murder that sent Buck Cole staggering back into the hall.

'And,' Bracken added, 'Stryker often talked about how he'd like to lift Nora Wade's skirts, too. Talked 'bout how I might help him.'

Buck Cole, reeling from Bracken's revelations, had one more blow to suffer.

'Stryker knew that he had no chance of Nora Wade's co-operation. So it didn't suprise me none when he . . .'

Buck Cole fled back inside the house, leaving the front door open. Eli Bracken grinned.

'I guess that means I can come in.'

He followed Cole to the den where he found the rancher sprawled on a cowhide sofa, pale as new milk. He continued with his cruel litany, ending, 'How did you figure your path was so smooth these last couple of years, Cole? Stryker would have had me dispatch the Wades as well, only for his hankering for Nora.'

Bracken poured himself a generous whiskey and slugged it down. He refilled the glass and pulled a chair in front of the rancher.

'Now, I know Stryker can't be hurt by none of this, Cole. But would you want Stryker's name to be blackened, and you in jail?'

'Me?'

'Well, you see, Cole, it wouldn't be no problem at all for me to twist things, and make it look like I was about to arrest Stryker for all those crimes he committed on your orders. I figure that airhead deputy of mine would recall how Stryker had confessed right there in front of him.'

Buck Cole gasped. 'Charlie Delap hasn't much brains, God knows. But he's an honest man. He wouldn't . . .'

Bracken's smile was leery. 'He would if I said I'd kill his wife and kids. And I would, too.' He held up his hands to stall Buck Cole's protest. 'The way I see it, Cole, you can boot me out and risk a US marshal seeing through my lies. Or . . .'

'Or?'

'For . . . say, two thousand dollars . . .' Buck Cole's pallor intensified. Bracken smirked cynically. 'Stryker'll keep his good name. And you won't go to jail.'

'*You're* blackmailing me?' the rancher raged in sudden anger.

Bracken sneered. 'Yeah. That's what I'm doing, sure enough. Just look on it as a contribution to my retirement fund, Cole.'

Buck Cole knew that, as a crooked lawman, Eli Bracken was shrewder and more clever than most of his kind. And it was likely that he could do as he said. Defeated, the rancher went to the wall safe, and came back with $2,000.

'This is not to save my skin, Bracken,' he growled. 'But I'll not have Stryker's name blackened. You utter a word after this and . . .'

Bracken greedily flicked the bills. Satisfied, he snorted, 'My lips are sealed.'

On leaving the Circle C, Eli Bracken clashed with Blackjack Ryan, still glancing over his shoulder.

'Seen a ghost, Blackjack?' the sheriff enquired. 'Looks that way.'

'What're you doin' out and 'bout at dead of

night?' Ryan questioned Bracken.

Bracken smiled slyly. 'Conducting business, of course.'

'What kinda business?'

'The kind of business that ain't your business, Blackjack.'

'To hell with you, then,' Ryan snapped surlily.

'Yeah, I guess that's where I'm bound for. But not just yet.' As Ryan had helped him a couple of times before, Bracken now roped him in on his last bit of mayhem around Hawk's Bend. 'Need fifty bucks, old friend?'

'Fifty? It's usually twenty.'

'I'm feeling generous. Want it or not?'

'What kinda loco question is that. Sure I want it.'

'Ain't you interested in what you have to do?' Bracken asked.

'Hah! For fifty bucks I'd carve up my dear, sweet old mother.'

The sheriff laughed. 'Guess you would too, Blackjack.'

'Where're we headed,' Ryan enquired as they set off.

'To collect a few friends.'

They rode into the night. Eli Bracken set to take his final revenge on the Wades.

As a long night neared its end, Ben Dalton saddled up and hit the trail at the first hint of daylight, hoping that the fear that had stalked him all night would not prove to have substance.

His eyes heavy as his energy drained away, Ned

Wade fell into a doze. His slide into sleep was unfortunate, because if he had remained alert for a few more minutes he'd have seen the men coming out of the predawn shadows at the side of the barn holding torches, as yet unlit. They were led by Eli Bracken.

Ben Dalton had ridden hard, eating up the trail at a breakneck pace, taking risks in the poor light. His fear for Nora Wade's safety became more acute with every second. He coaxed and scolded his horse in equal measure, and, in the main, except for a few lulls in pace, the horse responded to his urgency.

Bracken urged the passel of cut-throats he had assembled. 'Take it easy, fellas.'

'Ain't no one 'bout, Eli,' a toad of a man, whose help Bracken had frequently enlisted when dirty dealings were afoot, griped. 'It'll be all over 'fore them Wades'll know it.'

But the crooked sheriff held back a while longer to be sure that this, his last act of treachery, was not the one that would backfire on him. He had ridden his luck for three years knowing that sooner or later it would fizzle out. A time or two it nearly had, and he was going to wait for as long as it took to make sure that his luck held just one last time.

'What're we waitin' for, Eli?' another man asked nervously. 'It'll be light soon.'

'Yeah,' the toad griped. 'Frank's right. Let's light

these torches and burn them Wades out.'

Blackjack Ryan, feeling a sense of loyalty to Bracken on account of getting fifty dollars when the others had got only twenty, backed his benefactor. 'You all stop your whinin'. Eli will act when he's good and ready to.'

Bracken thought maybe he was being over-cautious. If Ned Wade had been on guard he'd have seen them for sure. Maybe not at first. But now, with the light turning to a pasty grey, he almost certainly would have. Bracken would have expected that after the events of the day before, Ned Wade would have kept watch. But then Ned Wade had long ago given up on life, leaving the providing to Nora, a duty she had performed well in very difficult circumstances. A pity, Bracken thought, that such a fine woman would have to be sacrificed. A pure waste, it was.

Edgily conscious of the brightening sky, Blackjack Ryan said, 'I reckon it's 'bout time at that, Eli.'

Bracken nodded. 'OK. Light your torches, fellas.'

Nora woke to see Randy, whom she had sleep in her room because of his distress the previous evening, tossing restlessly and moaning. He was having a nightmare. She went to him and rubbed his sweating brow. He woke briefly.

'It's all right, Randy,' she said. 'I'm right here.'

He smiled and settled back to sleep.

Nora went to the main room of the cabin, where she found Ned Wade asleep in his chair by the window. She fretted over his shallow breathing, and the flecks of dried blood on his lips. His lung sickness was getting rapidly worse. Observing her husband's unhealthy pallor, Nora Wade thought for the first time about being a widow. Guilt crowded in on her. Regret, too, for having held out against Buck Cole way beyond good sense.

'My cousin Frank wrote me about a new town starting up in Montana, Nora.' Ned Wade's words echoed back through time. 'We could settle with Cole and start up a store there.'

'Storekeepers?' she had scoffed. 'We're farmers, Ned. It's all we know.'

'We could learn,' he had pleaded.

Then the argument would drag, getting more heated with each bout, until days would go by without a word passing between them. Problems mounted. Ned got his first fit of coughing. A cold, that was all. It would pass. But it hadn't.

Looking now at her husband's narrow, hunched shoulders, bony hands, hollow eyes and pinched face, Nora knew that widder's weeds were in the offing.

'Ned,' she called softly. His weary, lifeless eyes opened sluggishly. 'You go to bed now. It's almost dawn.'

She was helping him out of his chair when she spotted movement in the shadows in the yard. The light was between night and day, and she thought at first that it was a trick of the light, until she saw the flare of a torch. Three more torches flared, and her heart raced with fear.

Ned Wade picked up on his wife's tension and his eyes flashed to the window. He smashed one of the windowpanes with his rifle and fired. One of the raiders spun. The torch he was bearing fell on him as he dropped and he became an instant inferno, howling like a wild animal as the flames devoured him. The nauseating stench of burning flesh filled the air.

'How many damn bullets has Wade got in that rifle,' Bracken swore, diving for cover under a fusilade.

Ned Wade had let his anger override his sense.

'Now!' Bracken hollered, on hearing the click of an empty gun.

They charged the house, and slung their torches with practised ease. The Wades were not the first homesteaders they had burned out. Two torches landed on the roof, and one sailed through the window past Wade. A can of kerosene followed the torch through the window. Fire mushroomed. Rain had been sparse in recent months. Sun and strong winds had dried the cabin walls tinder-dry. Flames raced up the walls, cutting off a passage to the bedroom.

'Randy!' Nora cried out.

Wade grabbed a bucket of water and threw it on the flames with little effect. Another torch crashed through the window. Outside, hoofs sounded as the arsonists lit out.

'Get out, Nora!' Wade shouted.

She resisted his shove to the door.

'Not without Randy!'

'I'll get the boy . . . our son, Nora,' Wade said.

He sprinted through the enclosing fire. He felt the searing heat on his skin. Thick smoke choked off his breath. His head spun. His eyes blurred. Randy was sitting up in bed wide-eyed, frozen. Ned Wade's legs buckled. His strength flooded out of him, leaving barely enough to help Randy out of the window to Nora's waiting arms.

'Come on, Ned,' she urged her husband, as he staggered back from the window.

'I won't fit through, Nora,' he said. He looked behind him at the flames sweeping towards him. 'And there's no way back.'

He reached out his hands to grasp Nora's.

'Remember what I said about you and Ben Dalton,' he gasped, and fell back into the smoke-filled room.

'Ned,' Nora screamed.

The instant he crested a hill overlooking the Wade homestead, Ben Dalton's heart lurched when he saw the flames engulfing the cabin. He spurred his horse, and rode helter-skelter.

From behind Nora Wade an arm grabbed Randy. She spun around to see Eli Bracken hoist him on to his horse.

'Tell Dalton that if he comes looking I'll kill the boy!' he warned.

Helpless, in hopeless desperation, Nora watched Eli Bracken ride off.

'Mom,' Randy screamed. 'Help me, Mom.'

CHAPTER THIRTEEN

Ben Dalton felt the weakness in his horse's legs and knew that he should draw rein on his headlong gallop. But seeing Eli Bracken ride off with Randy Wade in his clutches left Dalton with no choice but to push his horse even harder to try and cut off Bracken's escape.

Two riders wheeled to line up the approaching gunfighter in their rifle sights, but, riding low in the saddle, Dalton made a difficult target to nail. He also, in so far as his exhausted mount would allow him to, cut a weaving path that doubled the shooters' problems.

Dalton knew that the sensible thing to do would be to seek cover in the trees near the house and return fire, but Nora Wade's soulful cry at seeing Eli Bracken ride off with Randy tore at his heart. He'd be wasting his time shooting while riding at full gallop. And wasting much needed ammunition would be foolish also. There were four riders, and that meant four guns to his one. So when he started shooting, every bullet had to count.

Lead buzzed around Ben Dalton. The fire had taken a firm hold on the house, and that was an added urgency. Ned Wade was nowhere to be seen, and that could only mean one thing, surely. He was trapped inside the house. And with more and more of the structure ablaze, every second counted.

A bullet buzzed off Dalton's right stirrup, sending a shock wave along his leg, numbing it as far as his thigh. Another bullet whipped the hat from his head. The arsonists were getting his range. It was only a matter of time before he was downed.

The man now lining him up in his sights was none other than Blackjack Ryan, looking for another bite of the cherry. Dalton pulled on the reins just as Ryan's rifle spat. He felt the breeze of the bullet fan his forehead. He wheeled. Rifle hip-high, he fired. Ryan toppled from his horse, but he was not finished. He again tried to line Dalton up. The gunfighter's rifle blazed for a second time, and Blackjack Ryan was pitched into hell.

'Take the woman as a hostage,' the fleeing sheriff hollered.

Incensed, Ben Dalton cut loose with a yell that would have stood an Apache's hair on end. He charged headlong, his Winchester spitting.

'Shit!' one of the men yelled as a bullet spun off his saddle horn. 'I'm gittin'.'

A second man too, feeling the breeze of Ben Dalton's bullets, said, 'I ain't hangin' 'round neither.'

He swung his horse on his partner's tail, but was catapulted from his saddle as a bullet shattered his face and most of his head. The other rider did not get much further before he was downed by Dalton's deadly fire. The remaining arsonist, angry as a polecat, looked after Eli Bracken, by now well out of range from Dalton's gun.

'Bastard!' he swore, wasting time and lead on the rapidly vanishing sheriff. Realizing how useless his efforts for revenge on Eli Bracken were, with no mean skill he spun and fired at Dalton.

The gunfighter's horse vanished from under him, stumbling headlong as a bullet shattered his left leg. His rifle flew from his grasp as he tried to break his fall, before his fall broke him. He crashed to the ground. The wind was forced from his lungs, and the jarring of bones crippled him with pain. His six-gun spun out of its holster, leaving him weaponless and completely at the mercy of the remaining arsonist.

Nora Wade gathered her wits. She had to do something. The arsonist would kill Ben Dalton for certain. Ned was also inside the house, probably past help by now, but she had to try and get to him. Randy was still calling to her, but his cries were fading. Nora was finding it hard to grasp how she could have lost everything in a couple of minutes, because that was all that had elapsed since she had first seen the flare of the arsonists' torches.

Nora glanced about helplessly.

What could she do?

CHAPTER FOURTEEN

Nora's eyes came to rest on a discarded kerosene can near a shed. The can was upright. Did it contain kerosene? Sparks from the house carried on the wind had set light to the roof of the barn and sections of it were already falling to the ground. The flames had not fully taken hold, but in no time at all the structure would suffer the same fate as the house.

She picked up the can and shook it. The slosh of kerosene was heavenly music to Nora's ears. She looked to Ben Dalton. The arsonist was dismounting, smug in the knowledge that killing Dalton would now be trouble-free. He was taking his time, strolling to where Dalton lay, savouring his revenge. In seconds he would be standing over Ben Dalton, pulling a trigger.

The horror of Nora Wade's plan appalled her. But she could see no other way to prevent Ben Dalton's demise. Nora tore a strip from her skirts and soaked it with kerosene. She stuffed the rag into the neck of the can.

'Leave him be!' she ordered Ben Dalton's tormentor.

The man sneered. 'Now why would I wanna do that, ma'am?' His gaze settling on the can of kerosene, he scoffed: 'You ain't got the nerve.'

'I have the nerve, mister,' Nora promised him.

'I'm gamblin' that you ain't.'

The Bracken henchman levelled his six-gun on Ben Dalton.

'Then you've lost,' Nora murmured. She lit the rag from the burning debris of the barn. 'God forgive me,' she prayed. Nora hurled the can at the arsonist. On hitting the ground, the container split open and the burning kerosene splashed the man. He looked in horror as flames gushed on him. His howl of agony echoed across the range as the flames engulfed him. He pranced about in a desperate but useless attempt to shed his clothing. His hair caught fire and a ball of flame encircled his face and head. He staggered to a water trough to cool his agony. He fell into it face first, charred. Weak from the violence she had unleashed, faintness swept over Nora Wade. Ben Dalton took her in his arms, as she began to weep bitterly at the barbarity of her act. But his consolation had to be brief. He grabbed a blanket from his bedroll and soaked it in the water trough. He then wrapped the sodden blanket round his shoulders and head in a cowl and dived into the burning cabin.

Inside the house, flame was shooting every which way, and new gushes were flaring all the time. The smoke was molasses thick and tore at his lungs. As he danced across a floor erupting in flame, Dalton reckoned that he was getting a taste of hell. A ceiling beam crashed down behind him, missing him by inches. It fragmented and showered sparks everywhere, setting off new fires.

He dived into the bedroom just as a ragged hole opened in the roof, creating a down-draught which swept the flames to new heights of ferocity. His retreat was cut off. All he could do was drag Wade into a corner and watch the flames march steadily towards him, inch by murderous inch. There was nowhere to go.

He was trapped!

CHAPTER FIFTEEN

Circle C riders, led by Buck Cole, charged into the yard. The rancher leaped from his horse. 'One of my men saw what that cur Bracken did, Nora. Got here as soon as I could. Are Ned and Randy in there?'

'Ned and Ben Dalton. Eli Bracken snatched Randy.'

'Dalton, huh? Don't settle well with me to save his hide. But . . .' He ordered his men: 'Sling your ropes on that buckboard and haul it to that rise of ground behind the cabin. Rear end facing the cabin wall. Pronto!'

'What good will that do, Buck?' Nora questioned.

'The cabin is burning from the front,' the rancher reasoned. 'That means that if either Ned or Dalton is still alive, they must be at the rear of the cabin. Nowhere else they can be. So we've got to try and breach the rear wall. But . . .' he took Nora's hands in his to explain, 'Doing that, the whole damn structure might come tumbling. You want to take that risk, Nora?'

Nora said despondently, 'Guess whatever we do, there'll be a risk, Buck.'

The rancher hurried off after the Circle C crew who had made good progress. When they had hauled the wagon to where Buck Cole intended, he ordered: 'Put a couple of rocks under the front wheels.' The wagon's position secured, he further added: 'Now, two of you boys tie your ropes round those rocks, loop the other ends round your saddle horns and be ready to pull when I say so. The rest of you men get behind the wagon and shove like hell when it starts to roll. It'll need all the speed it can get up before hitting the cabin wall.'

This done, Buck Cole hailed the cabin.

'Ned? Dalton? If you can still hear me, there'll be a buckboard coming through the back wall of the cabin any second now,' he warned.

Almost spent, Ben Dalton clawed his way up the cabin wall to the window to see where the wagon was positioned, to try and gauge the path that it would take and where it would be likely to crash through the wall. Task completed, he slid back down the wall and tried with the last of his energy to drag Ned Wade away from where he reckoned the wall would be breached. But there were no certainties. A free-wheeling buckboard could change direction many times on the rocky ground, and in the end he might be moving into the section of the wall where the buckboard would smash through. All he could hope for was that when the buckboard started to roll, its run would not be too erratic. If that happened, the far section of the wall should bear the full brunt of the collision. But there was still no guarantee that the wall would crumble. And if it did, it might very well bring the remainder of the burning roof crashing down on them.

'OK, fellas,' Buck Cole hollered. 'Pull on those ropes!'

At first the weight of the wagon held the rocks firm.

'Tauten those ropes, dammit!' Cole bellowed.

The men on the horses tautened the ropes and pulled again. This time the rocks catapulted from under the wheels and the wagon began to roll. Cole, lending his shoulder with the rest of his men, shouted:

'Shove with all your might!'

Sluggish at first, the buckboard soon gained momentum and headed down the slope at a thunderous pace, careering wildly. The buckboard's shaft dragging on the ground changed the buckboard's direction all the time, first forcing it right, then left, then right again. The speeding wheels bounced every which way, and Cole feared that the buckboard would jack-knife and smash to smithereens. If that happened its impact against the cabin wall would be minimized, and would probably not be of sufficient force to breach the wall.

Nora grabbed the rancher's arm and held her breath as the shaft of the buckboard swung out to collide with a tree trunk. The shaft was snapped clean off. The wagon reared up wildly, balanced for a second on its front wheels, before becoming airborne. The wagon arced through the air and looked likely to crash through the roof rather than collide with the cabin wall. It bounced off a boulder and changed direction again. This time it looked set to miss the cabin completelely and simply break into pieces as it tumbled past on into the yard. It crashed down on its left-side front wheel. The wheel shattered, but the wheel's spokes set the wagon on its final path, straight in to the cabin wall with a terrific impact that shook the fire-damaged structure from end to end.

The impact was ferocious, sending Nora and the Circle C crew diving to the ground as chunks of the wagon and flaming debris rained down on them. One man cried out as a flying wheel smashed his leg. For a breathless moment the cabin wall held before crumbling. Men sprinted forward to haul Ned Wade and Ben Dalton free, just as the structure began to collapse in on itself in a fiery inferno.

Ben Dalton lay on the ground drawing in great heaving breaths. But Ned Wade lay still, his eyes empty. Nora came to kneel alongside her husband, and wept quietly.

'Sorry, Nora,' Buck Cole sympathized. 'I never

wanted for all this to happen. Stryker dead. Now Ned, too.'

Nora said, 'I guess it wouldn't have happened if I hadn't been so stubborn, Buck.'

'You can't blame yourself. You did what you thought was right.' The rancher's eyes were downcast when he said, 'I wronged you, Nora. Dalton, too. But you'll understand a man not wanting to admit to himself that the son he sired had a canker of badness in him.'

He looked about at the devastation and death, and sighed wearily.

'This surely is the devil's work, Nora.'

CHAPTER SIXTEEN

'Let me go!' Randy Wade demanded of Eli Bracken, fighting the sheriff's hold on him.

Bracken slapped the boy hard and warned: 'You keep riling me, boy. And so help me I'll drop you down a damn mineshaft!'

Randy Wade's eyes cast wildly about the hills. He had visited a mine with his pa when he was little (which at ten years of age he hadn't considered himself to be any more), and had been terrified by the tight, airless confines of the mine, and the million undefined slithers and squeaks in the dark just outside the range of the lamp his pa had carried. It turned out to be what his ma had called another wild-goose chase. Pa got loco ideas from time to time. He'd get it in his head that the old mineshafts dotting the hills around the valley held riches missed out on by the army of prospectors and mining outfits. There was never any gold, but that didn't stop Pa dreaming. Now, his visit to the mine with his pa brought home the full horrors of Eli Bracken's threat.

Bracken, a cruel-hearted man, took pleasure in Randy Wade's fright and turned the screw even harder still.

'Maybe leave you right here for a mountain cat to eat, boy.'

Randy hammered his small fists on Eli Bracken's chest. The crooked sheriff slapped him hard again, and the boy tumbled backwards.

'I told you what I'll do if you give me any more trouble,' Bracken snarled. 'Now, I've gotta do some fast thinking, so you be still as a darn church mouse, boy.'

Randy went to cower behind a boulder. 'Ma . . . Pa, where are you?' he wept.

Eli Bracken had not gone very far when his problems came home to roost. Though it had seemed a good idea at the time to grab the boy, he was now having second thoughts about taking him along. The boy had slowed him down. He should have ridden like the wind to town, collected his ill-gotten gains and hit the trail for distant parts before news of his dirty deeds reached Hawk's Bend. Once that happened, it was likely that the good and righteous would form a posse to hunt him down. He should never have given in to the temptation to burn the Wades out. Once he'd shaken down Buck Cole, he should have had the sense to leave well enough alone. He had let spite and greed rule his judgement, and now he might have to pay a hefty price for his self-indulgence.

There was also Ben Dalton to worry about. A

posse he'd have the savvy to dodge, but not Dalton. Twenty years on the trails, living a minute at the time, would have taught him all the tricks. The fact that the gunfighter had survived for so long was proof positive that he had learned well.

But his biggest worry of all was that he might have to leave Hawk's Bend with nothing more than the wad of Cole dollars in his pocket. A nice penny, sure enough. But chicken-feed compared to the riches he had stashed back in town. His dilemma was, should he ride with what he had in his pocket, and probably save his neck from a noose in the long run? Or hide out until dark, slip back into town, and grab those bulging valises?

Eli Bracken sweated.

Hide out where? It would have to be some place safe. It would be a long day with a snotty kid, but if events did not pan out in his favour, the boy would be a valuable bargaining chip. There were Circle C line shacks higher up which he could make for. The problem was that at any moment a Circle C rannie could drop by and find him. Maybe the rannie would have heard of the ruckus at the Wade place. Maybe he would not have heard, too. Sometimes the rannies were gone for days at a time. But finding him with the boy, he'd ask questions. Whatever a man got up to on tough range might be considered his business. But snatching a boy would go far beyond the bounds of permissible behaviour. That ruled out a line shack, Bracken thought glumly.

So what was left?

A cave close to the Wade homestead came to mind, roomy enough. There was, he recalled, an exit from the cave through a narrow aperture which led to the ridge above. An escape route, if needed. Not a very pleasant one, though, tight-fitting and probably filled with the menace of rattlers. But if events panned out in such a way that beggars could not be choosers . . . .

Of course, if he had to use that escape route, it would leave him without a horse.

The plus in the plan might be that the cave was within spitting distance of the Wade homestead. Now who would expect, after the ruckus he had started, that he would hide out on the Wades' doorstep? Everyone would expect him to eat up trail to the border. With luck he could hold out in the cave until darkness came. Then he would slip into town, collect his loot, and make fast tracks out of the territory.

And if bad luck dogged him, Randy Wade would be his hostage.

His plan formulated, Eli Bracken doubled back on his trail, pausing every now and then to scatter his sign by drawing a sapling branch over his back trail, and to monitor the trail ahead and behind for any sign of pursuit.

As he drew near to the Wade homestead, Bracken tied Randy to a tree and gagged him to stop him calling out. It was unlikely that his voice would reach the Wade house, but why take the chance. From the ridge above the cave which was to be his hidy-hole, the Hawk's Bend sheriff eyed the burning homestead. He'd have expected it to be ashes by now, but the structure was tougher than it looked, and a change in wind direction was holding the flames to the front of the cabin.

Men, obviously Circle C hands led by Buck Cole, were hauling a wagon to the rise of ground behind the burning house. Their plan of action was clear. They intended to ram the cabin's rear wall and force open an escape hatch.

He could see no sign of Ben Dalton. Bracken's heart skipped a beat. Was Dalton already on his tail? His panic was momentary. Dalton was sweet on Nora Wade. He'd not desert her. Then his panic was back. The brat was Nora Wade's sole reason for living these last couple of years. Maybe she had prevailed on Dalton to give immediate chase? Ned Wade had been trapped inside the cabin – a goner for sure. So there would be no point in Dalton hanging around trying to rescue him.

And maybe Dalton had caught lead?

When he'd lit out, Dalton had been under heavy fire. Then Bracken's thoughts took another track. If Buck Cole was preparing to breach the back wall of the cabin . . . . Had Ben Dalton been loco enough to try and rescue Ned Wade? And if he had, was Buck Cole forgiving enough to want to save his hide? He waited until the charging buck-board breached the cabin wall to have his thoughts confirmed, when they hauled Ben Dalton and Ned Wade from the inferno. Clearly, Ned Wade had not made it. But Ben Dalton had, and that handed him a problem he could have done without.

He untied Randy Wade from the tree, but left him gagged. He made his way to the cave. Randy's eyes glowed with fear when he saw their destination, and he fought Bracken tigerishly.

'Get inside that damn cave, boy,' the crooked lawman snarled, and laid the back of his hand across Randy's head. He shoved him inside the gloomy cave. 'I've taken all the antics I'm going to take from you, you hear me?'

Eli Bracken's eye caught sight of a dead rattlesnake. He picked it up and dangled it in front of Randy, vibrating his tongue and hissing to mimic an angry rattler. Randy went rigid with fright. Taking pleasure in the youngster's terror, Bracken heightened it further by throwing the dead rattler at the boy. Randy went purple with a surpressed scream.

'Just as well I put that gag on you,' Bracken snorted. 'Otherwise we'd have this whole rock down on us by now.'

On seeing the stream of urine down Randy Wade's legs, Bracken growled.

'Damn! You ain't going to mess yourself too, are ya? This cave ain't big enough for the stench of a privy!' The Hawk's Bend badge-toter grabbed Randy and held his thin frame effortlessly aloft. 'If you ever want to see that ma of yours again, you'll not give me any more trouble.'

Bracken picked up a rock and threw it into the darkness. Its clatter echoed back, mixed with other sounds. Slithering, rattling sounds. He held Randy face to face. 'There's plenty of live rattlers back there. I'll toss you right on top of them if you so much as squeak!'

The sheriff carefully used the sapling branch to scatter hoof-and boot-prints from the entrance to the cave. Satisfied that he was as safe as he could possibly make himself, he settled down to wait until darkness fell.

It would be a long wait with a pesky boy, but he resigned himself. He had no choice if he wanted to get his mitts on those two bulging valises back in town. He had not yet begun to think seriously about what he would do with Randy Wade once his usefulness was over. He could turn him loose, but not too soon. Because, dim-witted though he was, he might just be able to tell Dalton and Buck Cole the trail he took. There was no way of knowing what kind of knowledge was inside the youngster's head. And if he took him too far, and then cut him loose, it was likely he would perish. Best, Bracken figured, to kill the boy. He had never killed a kid before. But if it was a toss-up between keeping his ill-gotten gains and Randy Wade, well, there would be no contest.

Of that he was certain.

CHAPTER SEVENTEEN

Ben Dalton lay gulping air. His head spun. His belly heaved. He lay exhausted. Spent. But as angry as a riled cougar with the man who had wreaked such carnage.

Buck Cole helped Nora Wade up from her husband's side.

'It's no good you distressing yourself so, Nora,' the rancher said. 'Ned's gone. Now we've got to think about the living.' He ordered his men: 'Head back to the ranch. Form a posse. Hunt Bracken down before he reaches the border. But be careful that the boy comes to no harm. Send a barouche for Mrs Wade to take her back to the Circle C.'

Buck Cole added a chilling addendum:

'When you snare Eli Bracken, hang him!' The Circle C riders mounted up with grim purpose, and rode like the wind.

Nora Wade said, 'I thank you for your kindness, Buck. But—'

'Nora,' he shushed, 'we've been locking horns for too long. It's time to settle this range.' Wearily, he looked out across the undulating grassland. 'It's taken too much blood to grow this damn grass, Nora.' His gaze held hers. 'We've both got dead to bury. I say, let's do it, and move on.'

Nora looked at the ruination all round her. She saw in her mind's eye the dream which she and Ned Wade had dreamed twelve years previously when they had stopped their wagon at Bowie Creek and had first set eyes on the rich farmland spreading out from the creek to where, on that very day, they had decided their home would stand. Eagerly, Ned had established that the land he planned to plough was free range and filed his claim.

At first Buck Cole was supportive of his new neighbours. The rancher believed in strong family life, and saw the Wades as welcome additions, who would produce the offspring needed in time to come to continue what had been started. Stryker Cole was only a boy then, of a nature that was quite loveable. He became a frequent visitor to the Wade house, and when Randy was born often took the new arrival from under Nora's feet when chores, of which there were always too many, had to be done.

They went to the Circle C for dinner. And Buck Cole and his wife often partook of their simple fare, too. They were golden times, when happiness seemed endless. Then, one awful day, Mary Cole got on the wrong side of a bad-tempered mustang and got kicked in the head. She took a week to die, and it was a week in which a gloom rolled in over the range. It hadn't since lifted.

Buck Cole became a broken, angry and bitter man. In the absence of his doting mother, Stryker Cole's nature took a turn for the worse too. He became surly and bad-tempered, and took to mocking and taunting Randy, until later his behavior became hostile and utterly cruel. Nora had spoken to Buck Cole about Stryker's carry-on, but the rancher was imprisoned by his loss too much to notice or care.

Stryker Cole had begun to seek the company of the likes of Blackjack Ryan and a whole bevy of hardcases and no-goods who frequented the saloons of Hawk's Bend and further afield, and was slowly but irrevocably sucked into the whirlpool of malice and skulduggery which was part and parcel of being associated with such dregs.

Stryker, Nora noticed, began to look differently at her. She began to read in his eyes the lust in his heart; the lust which had eventually become uncontrollable and had led to the awful events visited on her and Buck Cole. But good had also come out of evil. Buck Cole seemed to have shed the strangling lethargy which had gripped him since the death of his beloved Mary. And he was once again the Buck Cole she and Ned knew and loved.

Nora said, 'Buck, I thank you for your Christian
kindness.' She smiled sadly. 'Though it's come a
mite late, it's still mighty welcome.' Her chin
jutted, and her eyes lit with a fire of determinaton
and resolve. 'I have decided to make Ned Wade's
dream come true, Buck.'

'You can't work this place on your own, Nora,'
the rancher said.

'I'm not fool enough to think I could,' she
replied. 'But with your help, and . . .' Her gaze
settled on Ben Dalton.

Buck Cole followed her gaze. A fiery rejection
of Nora's thinking sprang to his lips, but he held
his tongue. He had interfered too much in Wade
affairs. And, besides, Dalton had simply come to
a lady's defence, the way any half-decent man
would have. He had checked Eli Bracken's tale
about Stryker's hankering for Nora Wade with
the men, promising no adverse sanctions if the
truth was spoken. He had got book and verse
about his son's promise to one day take his pleasure from Nora Wade, whether she was willing or
not. His one mistake had been that when
Bracken had come calling the night before to
blackmail him, had he faced up to what he knew
in his heart to be true, he should have horse-
whipped him.

He had played his part in Stryker's downfall, and
his guilt would stalk him to his grave. His retreat
from the world on his wife's death had allowed the
seeds of badness to be sown in what had been a

good heart. Now he had many mistakes to put right. His time, however long or short it might be, would be devoted to setting right the wrongs he had let take root.

Nora said, 'You're welcome to the water in the creek, Buck. As much as you want. There's plenty for both our needs.'

In that second, on Nora Wade's offer, Buck Cole's journey back to good neighbourliness lost most of the dark dread and isolation it had held for him.

'Obliged, Nora,' the rancher said, in the kind of soft voice that Nora had not heard for a long, long time.

Buck Cole went to his horse and took a bottle of Kentucky rye from his saddlebag. He returned and helped Ben Dalton to his feet. He handed the shaky-legged gunfighter the bottle.

'Get some of that down your gullet, Dalton,' he said. 'It'll have you dancing in no time at all.'

Dalton, somewhat surprised, took the bottle and slugged. The rancher's claim for the rye was correct. It rushed down to his toes, and washed away the muzziness in his head with equal alacrity.

'We'll bury Ned here, Nora. At a place of your choosing.' He smiled warmly. 'Then we'll all head back to the Circle C to make plans for rebuilding the Wade farm.'

Ben Dalton handed the bottle which now had lots of clear glass to Buck Cole and said, 'I've got a boy to find, and a killer to bring to book.'

'You're in no fit state,' Cole said. 'The boys will snare him.'

Ben Dalton said, 'Maybe. Maybe not. But I reckon Eli Bracken hasn't survived this long by chance. He's a planning kind of man.'

'What do you mean, Ben?' Nora asked.

Dalton asked the rancher: 'Bracken's been on the take for a long time, right?'

The Circle C boss confirmed: 'Yeah. Must have a really hefty poke from his dirty dealings. Including two thousand of my dollars.'

Dalton and Nora fixed their gaze on Buck Cole.

'Long story, which I'll get 'round to telling one day.'

Ben Dalton opined: 'I figure that burning you out, Nora, was Bracken's last act of spite before hitting the trail. Now I also reckon that Bracken, with a passel of no-goods in tow, did not come calling toting his ill-gotten gains. Which means that his poke is still stashed back in town.'

Grimly, Ben Dalton said: 'And there's no way that Bracken is going to let his poke slip from his grasp.'

'Hanging around could put a noose round his neck,' Buck Cole said.

'Even with a rope dangling,' Ben Dalton opined, 'Eli Bracken will risk getting his hands on his booty.'

The rancher was doubtful. 'You figure that he's still in these parts, Dalton?'

Ben Dalton gazed into the distance. 'That's the way I figure. Have to borrow your horse,' he told Cole.

He swung into the saddle, and rode away.

CHAPTER EIGHTEEN

Ben Dalton rode away from the Wade homestead with a heavy heart. There was more killing to be done, and it seemed that there always would be. He had forgotten for a short time, since he had met Nora Wade at the creek, that a man had to live with his reputation, that dreaming, as he had, that it could ever be different had been the act of a fool. The West was grudging in allowing a man to change his spots. He had seen the way Buck Cole looked at Nora, too. It was not in a way that meant a man desired a woman for the sake of his own gratification. There was more. His look was warm and soft and caring. He'd not stand between Nora and Cole. He had nothing to offer Nora Wade but good intentions. And the West was awash with women who had put their trust in good intentions, and had lived to regret their foolishness. He'd not let Nora down. But she would always have to live with the fear that one day a man seeking to outdraw the fast-gunned Ben Dalton would come calling. And those would be terrible minutes in which Nora might again face widowhood. It would be a life lived a breath at a time, and he would not inflict that kind of existence on the woman with whom he had fallen deeply in love.

Nora watched Ben Dalton ride away, her heart smothered by fear for his safety. Buck Cole, though he had harboured thoughts of, in time, asking Nora to be his wife, let them go. With Ned Wade dead, there was clearly only one man who would figure in Nora Wade's life from now on.

'He'll be fine, Nora,' the rancher said.

Nora blushed. Cole smiled.

'Nora,' he said, 'I'm not about to deny that I'd thought about asking you to wed me after Ned passed on . . .'

Nora's blush deepened.

'God knows Ned had expressed his worry about you being on your own many times, before that damn creek got in the way.' The rancher's shoulders slumped. 'But I know that if you married me now it would be because Ben Dalton wouldn't have you.' He grinned. 'Not that you have any worries on that score, I reckon. Dalton will be as eager to frolic as a spring lamb.'

'Buck Cole,' Nora wailed. 'Have you no hold on your tongue.'

'Talking straight has been my hallmark for too long for me to start changing my ways now,' he said. 'And you know what I said is true.'

'I do not!'

'Oh, yes you do. Ain't nothing as off-putting in a

woman as false modesty!' Cole took Nora's hands in his. 'You had hard times, Nora. And to my shame I played my part in making them so. Ned was a good man, who just couldn't take being an invalid. Might seem a cruel thing to say, but I reckon he's better off now.

'But you've got a life to live. I wish it was under my roof for the time I have. But it won't be. That's not to say that I can't help you and Ben Dalton get this place back on its feet. And that's what I want to do, Nora. If you'll let me.'

'Buck,' she squeezed his hand in hers, 'I'm not sure right now where my roots will be. But if they're here, I'll be glad and grateful for any help you'll be of a mind to give me.'

Eli Bracken watched as the Circle C crew rode hell for leather across the valley, their horses' noses pointed towards the border. The sight calmed his nerves some, but not fully. Because among their ranks he could not see Ben Dalton, and that meant only one thing. It was as he suspected; Dalton had not fallen for his trickery and was on a solo mission to hunt him down. His nerves rawer than ever, he scampered back to the cave, glancing wildy about him, feeling the burn of eyes on him – his imagination working overtime, he hoped.

His nerves jangled when, nearing the cave, a trickle of shale clattered down from the ridge above. He dived into a cluster of boulders, six-gun in hand, cursing that he had not brought his rifle with him when he left the cave to reconnoitre; a handgun would be no use at all if Ben Dalton was on the ridge.

He waited, his eyes wild. It was absolutely still, and that jangled Bracken's nerves even more. Had Dalton spotted him? Was he playing cat and mouse with him? Was that a shadow near that tree to the right of the ridge? He swiftly changed position. A shooter behind the tree would have a perfect bead on him. The urge to call out became almost unbearable. Eli Bracken liked to taunt and tease his victims, but he did not like being on the receiving end of such treatment himself.

How long should he wait before breaking for the cave? He thought about the aperture that led up out of the cave to the ridge. Maybe right now Ben Dalton was going the other way, down into the cave to rescue Randy Wade.

'You've got to get those nerves under control, Eli,' Bracken scolded himself. 'You're shaking like the last leaf on a fall tree.'

He forced himself to reason. There was no way, except by pure chance, that Dalton could have stumbled on his hidy-hole this fast. The last time he looked, which was – Bracken checked his pocket watch – only twenty minutes ago, Ben Dalton was gasping for breath, having just been rescued from the fire. However, no doubt Dalton was a man used to fast recovery. But could he get on board a horse and find him that fast? Never, was Eli Bracken's conclusion. The shale had been disturbed by some wild animal, or had simply become loose with the erosion of time.

Except by pure chance.

The phrase haunted Bracken. There was no doubting the sour turn his luck had taken. But had it gone that bad?

You can't hunker down all day, he told himself. If Dalton ain't on the ridge, he could happen by at any second.

That reasoning solved his dilemma. He sprinted to the cave in a crouched run. Arriving in one piece, he was now certain that Ben Dalton had not been on the ridge. But maybe he was already in the cave? He hugged the edge of the entrance, his thoughts about Dalton entering the cave through the aperture from the ridge raising his fear to new heights.

'Kid,' he called. 'You hear me?'

There was no response.

'Kid,' he called more urgently. 'Answer me or . . .'

Damn! He had gagged the kid. How could he answer him. But he could hear him.

'Kid, step forward to where I can see you.'

Haggard way beyond his years by fright, Randy Wade came to the mouth of the cave.

'You alone?'

Randy nodded.

'Sure?'

He nodded again.

' 'Cause if your fooling me, it'll go hard with you, boy.'

Eli Bracken edged into the cave an inch at a time, still alert, letting his eyes adjust to its murky interior. Slowly his nerves stopped jangling. He decided that he had had his last trip outside the cave before nightfall. He began to think about the bundles of dollar bills in the valises stuffed under his floorboards, and the pleasures and position those dollars would bring him in South America. He began to relax, but only for a short spell. A trick of light created an image of a dangling rope on the cave wall – at least that's what it looked like to him.

Eli Bracken's blood chilled.

CHAPTER NINETEEN

Ben Dalton, convinced that Eli Bracken had not gone far from the scene of his crime, examined every foot of terrain due south from the Wade homestead, the direction in which he had last seen Bracken heading. He could, of course, have changed direction. But if he was wrong and Bracken had, as the Circle C riders figured, beaten a trail for the border, he'd soon see sign to confirm that. But he was still counting on the twisted lawman's greed being too keen to have him leave all that loot he had stored up behind him. Most men, faced with a dangling noose, would have saved their necks first. However, the fact that Eli Bracken had put the squeeze on Buck Cole when he could have been long gone, showed him to be a man of insatiable greed: a greed that amounted to a compulsion; a compulsion Ben Dalton hoped would be Eli Bracken's undoing.

An hour into his search, Dalton began to think that his assessment of the crooked sheriff's intentions had been wrong. Perhaps he was the fool, and not the Circle C outfit riding the border trail. But would Bracken make tracks for the border with Randy in tow? Unlikely, was Dalton's opinon. The boy would slow him too much. Had he dumped Randy somewhere, and left the youngster wandering around in all sorts of danger? Ben Dalton figured that doing so would not give Eli Bracken any sleepless nights, but would he just turn Randy Wade loose? Would he risk the boy making his way home, or meeting up with a traveller and pointing out Bracken's direction?

Dalton reckoned not.

Ben Dalton did not want to think about the other possibility. That Eli Bracken had murdered the boy. That, he reckoned, would be a suffering too great for Nora Wade to bear.

Frustrated, Ben Dalton drew rein and took time out to marshal his thoughts. He recalled all that he had learned from the old Cheyenne who had taught him the trick of sleeping with a cocked six-gun, and he began to see sign that was not there before. A snapped shoot, broken in a way that pointed the direction in which the rider had passed; its fresh sap and clean bark telling him that it was a recent break. The scrawl of a spur on a boulder through a narrow gap, standing out clear against the weathered rock around it. Wet leaves in a patch of undergrowth off the trail, when nearby plants and scree were dry. Urine, maybe? And a trail whose dust bore an artistic quiver to it. The sign of a man covering his hoof imprints. Fresh horse-droppings with evidence of oats, meaning that the horse was livery-fed and not a horse travelling a trail and dependent on range grass.

'No matter how careful a man is, he cannot pass without leaving sign,' the old Cheyenne had told Dalton. 'Read a man's sign right, and it will lead you to him.'

He was not an Indian, and Ben Dalton knew that he could never hope to read sign as an Indian would. Still, he figured that he had seen enough sign to tell him that Eli Bracken was still around. But where?

'Go back,' the Cheyenne had told Dalton, 'to the start of a man's trail. Begin there. Be patient. The start of a man's journey will take you to the end of that journey, too.'

Dalton, smothering his anxiety, did as the Cheyenne had told him. He followed the fancy pattern of dust in the trail to its end. Then he doubled back and retraced all the signs he had seen, holding a tight rein on his urge to race ahead.

CHAPTER TWENTY

The trail led to a spot overlooking the Wade homestead. Nora Wade was leaving in the barouche
which Buck Cole had sent for, under the rancher's
caring and gentle attention. A fresh mound of
earth marked Ned Wade's grave. A duo of Circle C
rannies were placing a crude timber cross on the
mound. They then mounted up and acted as
Nora's escort. Dalton watched the barouche roll
across the fertile range, expertly guided by Buck
Cole, until a dip in the terrain took it out of sight.
Nora Wade, he reckoned, was on her way to her
new home at the Circle C. He was both bitter and
disappointed at the turn of events. But good sense
soon took over, and Ben Dalton knew that, heart-
breaking as it was, Nora Wade's journey and
present company would be the best for her.

Meanwhile, he had a killer to find.

Eli Bracken had not heard Ben Dalton's careful
approach to the southern rim of the ravine in
which his hidy-hole was situated. However,

instincts as sharp as a shark's tooth, honed through much mayhem in a long career of skulduggery, kicked in. A cold sweat trickled down his spine. He crept to the cave entrance and let his eyes drift across the ravine. He saw nothing, but believed in his instincts. He lay flat on the ground, rifle primed, its sights continuously sweeping the ravine. Nervous, he puffed on one of his stinking cheroots.

Ben Dalton, too, had needle-sharp instincts for danger. And in the seconds before Eli Bracken reacted to the trickle of sweat on his spine, the gunfighter's hackles quivered. Buck Cole's stallion, which Ben Dalton had borrowed, was reacting, Dalton would bet, to the scent of a mare on the curl of wind coming up out of the ravine. He had not been spotted. If he had been, he would not still be sitting in his saddle. Accepting his stroke of luck, he vanished off the horizon a mere breath before Eli Bracken came to the mouth of the cave.

Dalton quickly distanced himself to a meadow of lush grass well away from the mare's scent to avoid the stallion alerting Bracken to his presence. He took time to calm the horse, and waited until the horse's appetite for the lush grass overcame the mare's scent, and the stallion began to chew. Then he made his way back on foot to the ravine, pausing at its edge to scout the rocky enclave. His eyes went to the ridge, though as yet he was not aware of the cave below it. He had not seen the cave on his way through the ravine. It was well hidden. The approach to it was through a pair of leaning boulders that kept the secret of the cave beyond.

The ridge was the highest point, and it was to there that Ben Dalton made his cautious way. Before starting out, he discarded his hat and spurs. He also unbuckled his gunbelt, and took off his boots. He stuffed his six-gun in his trousers, and filled his pocket with the bullets from the gunbelt. Most men seeking a quarry ditched their spurs and gunbelt – spurs jangled, and the bullets in a gunbelt reflected light. But few ditched their hats or boots. And that was a mistake that had cost many men their lives. Because when crouched and moving through uneven terrain like the ravine, it would be next to impossible for a man always to gauge the distance between the top of his head and the top of his hat. Boots slipped and scraped – stockinged feet did not. With an adversary of Eli Bracken's ilk, one mistake would be all it would take to seriously disadvantage a hunter. His lariat he took with him. Not that he had, as yet, formulated any specifc plan. But past experience had taught him that a rope was sometimes as essential as a gun.

Ben Dalton progessed inch by inch, carefully and astutely weighing up all his options before making his next move, cautiously gauging distance between his present cover and the pitfalls ahead. A sudden glint of light directed his attention to the leaning boulders. Sun reflecting off a gun barrel? Or just the natural tricks of light found in rocky terrain? He belly-crawled to a point near the boulders and studied the lie of the land. He guessed that there might be a hidden cave beyond the boulders. Sniffing the air, Dalton put his sense of smell to work. A scent of tobacco: Mexican cheroot, he reckoned. And the odour of sour sweat. There was someone in the cave, and he was betting that it was Eli Bracken. Cleverly, he had chosen a hidy-hole right on the Wades' doorstep. Who would have expected that!

Watching every single pebble his passage might dislodge, Ben Dalton made his way to the ridge, keeping a tight rein on his urge to cut corners. It was slow and tedious progress. As he edged up to higher ground he saw the cave, and Eli Bracken hugging its entrance. The heat was beginning to build in the ravine. It would soon boil, and the light would hurt a man's eyes and haze his vision. The cave would be cooler, giving Bracken a distinct advantage.

Ben Dalton knew that he would have to act soon.

CHAPTER
TWENTY ONE

Although he could see no sign of trouble, Eli Bracken's nerves refused to settle. Maybe he was overwrought and allowing his imagination to spook him. But he didn't think so. He had no call to distrust his instincts. They had saved his hide too many times in the past to ignore them now. What should he do? Show himself? Risk drawing fire to pinpoint the lurker he was sure was around? It was not a thought that appealed to him. All his life he had killed by stealth, when there was little or no risk to his skin. But, somehow, this time, Bracken felt that to survive his present predicament, risk would be an inherent part of the game.

Reaching the ridge, Ben Dalton was unsure of what his next move would be, until his leg sank through a patch of unruly undergrowth. He cautiously parted the straggling bushes, and saw the opening into the cave. He peered carefully along the sloping track, taking only a couple of seconds to examine it. A down-draught from the strong breeze sweeping the ridge might alert Bracken to his presence. He thought about negotiating the slope, but saw a plethora of dangers in that plan. The track might narrow and he could get stuck, and become a sitting target for Bracken's gun. There was also the very real danger of sliding into a nest of rattlers. And even if there were no snakes, and if the track was wide enough all the way down, there was no way that he could negotiate it silently. The deeper he went, the poorer the light would be, and a mere pebble rattling down the duct would alert Eli Bracken to danger.

So what use could he make of the opening?

Smoke!

Recent rain had dampened the ridge's scrub and scree. If he could ignite it, it would give lots of smoke. He gathered together bundles of scrub and scree and stuffed them down into the opening as far as he could safely reach, praying that he would not feel the bite of fangs. His luck held. He struck a lucifer and tried to set fire to the scrub. Several attempts later it began to smoulder. Dalton used his coat to direct the breeze on to the embryonic fire. It flared. He then used his coat to trap the smoke and direct it down into the cave. He grinned. It was thick and acrid.

In the cave, Randy Wade's coughing-bout was the first hint of trouble for Eli Bracken. He looked back into the cave to where the boy was fast disappearing in the billowing smoke coming from the opening from the ridge. Thick, acrid, breath-snatching smoke was filling the cave. The choking smoke built swiftly, fed by plentiful supplies of damp scrub. It quickly filled every inch of breathable space. Eli Bracken now knew that his instincts had been right. But it was a pity they had not alerted him to the one possibility that he had not counted on.

Smoke!

CHAPTER
TWENTY TWO

The cave filled with noxious fumes. The breeze curling down off the ridge swept the cave entrance, preventing the smoke from escaping quickly enough, and there would be plenty of scrub on the ridge to keep the smoke going for as long as it took. In desperation, Bracken began shooting up the aperture, hoping that a lucky bullet would catch Ben Dalton. But the gunfighter, expecting such a move, remained clear of the opening. His concern was for Randy Wade. His small lungs would quickly fill with smoke.

Realizing that he was wasting his bullets, Eli Bracken, choking for breath, knew that he had to get out of the cave. Should he take the boy as a hostage? If he did it would slow him. But then if Randy Wade was on board his horse, it would pose all sorts of problems for Dalton. Any shooting would carry the risk of hitting the boy. And if the gunfighter were to bring down his horse, the end result in the rock-strewn ravine would almost certainly be the same. The kid would have a thousand chances of splitting open his skull. Besides, he could not hold on to the mare for much longer. Sensing fire, she was ready to bolt.

Deciding that his chances of slipping Ben Dalton's trap were best served by having Randy Wade as a hostage, Bracken grabbed the boy and mounted up. The excited horse bucked. The sheriff fought to get the mare under control, and mercilessly applied his spurs. The mare charged from the cave. The risk of being thrown was very real, but Bracken knew that if he were to survive the next couple of minutes, risks would have to be taken.

On hearing the mare's protest, Ben Dalton suddenly found a use for his lariat. He looped the rope around a fat-bellied boulder and dropped rapidly down the face of the ridge, praying that he would be in time to stop Eli Bracken dead in his tracks. Because if he escaped with Randy as a hostage, he would enjoy the upper hand. Shooting with Randy on board Bracken's horse would be too risky. A stray bullet or a spill from the horse could prove equally fatal. So his hastily concocted plan to nail the crooked lawman had one chance to work, and one chance only.

Bursting from the cave, Eli Bracken's eyes popped when he was confronted by Ben Dalton dangling in mid-air, like an avenging angel. His legs encircled Bracken in a leg-lock that yanked him from the saddle. It was with relief that Dalton saw Randy Wade fall on the sandy soil at the cave entrance. Dropping to the ground, the gunfighter shouted: 'Hide, Randy!' The boy scampered off into the rocks.

Quick to recover, Eli Bracken flashed his six-gun. Dalton's unshod foot shot out to catch the crooked sheriff on the jaw with only minimum effect. But it was enough to unbalance Bracken as he sought to stand up. The gunfighter's fist followed, catching Bracken full force on the side of the head. He crashed back on to the ground. His arm collided with a jagged stone, loosening his grip on the .45. Bracken kicked out at Dalton's legs, bringing him down. He sprang on the gunfighter, the blade of a hunting knife reflecting the sun. Dalton rolled aside, missing Bracken's blade by a breath. He corkscrewed up and looped his arm around the sheriff's throat in an armlock. Bracken gagged, but fought tigerishly. His elbow shot back into Dalton's gut, forcing him back. Bracken reacted swiftly and lunged at Dalton. The gunfighter got a leg up and into Bracken's midriff. Bracken sailed over him, and Ben Dalton heard the sheriff's agonized gasp as he landed on his own knife. He rolled over, his quivering fingers clutching at the hilt of the knife which was all that was showing out of his belly. Blood gushed through the deep and ragged wound. Bracken shuddered. His eyes rolled. And he was still.

Randy Wade ran to Ben Dalton's arms. When he

had calmed the boy Dalton said: 'Time to get you home to your ma, Randy.'

Nora Wade came running when Ben Dalton and Randy Wade rode up, for a tearful reunion with her son.

'Will you accept my hospitality, Dalton?' Buck Cole asked.

'I'd be grateful for a hot tub and a good meal,' Dalton said.

'Whatever you need is yours,' the rancher generously responded.

Ben Dalton put his hand inside his shirt, and pulled out a wad of dollar bills. He handed them to the rancher.

'This is your property, Cole.'

Stunned by an honesty he had not expected, Buck Cole promised: 'This will go to rebuilding the Wade homestead.'

Dalton said, 'I don't think there'll be any need for that, sir.'

Buck Cole did not understand Ben Dalton's words until the next morning when Nora Wade came hammering on his bedroom door before first light.

'Ben's gone,' she said, distressed. 'Why would he leave like a thief in the night, Buck? I don't understand.'

Buck Cole reckoned he did. Ben Dalton saw no future for Nora with him, and had given her the chance to settle down at the Circle C; a chance she would never have if he stayed around. In the weeks that followed, Buck Cole knew that gentle, kind and loving as he might be to Nora Wade, he never had a chance in hell of stepping into Ben Dalton's shoes. If he asked Nora to marry him, he reckoned that the chances of her saying yes were pretty good. But instead he changed his will to favour Nora Wade and Ben Dalton. The Circle C would be in good hands when he was gone. Then he hired a Pinkerton detective to find Ben Dalton.

'It'll take time,' the rancher told Nora, as her eyes danced like he had never seen them dance except when Ben Dalton was around. 'But one day you'll look up and Ben Dalton will be riding across Circle C range into your waiting arms, Nora.'

Nora Wade hugged Buck Cole to her. Darn, he thought, why do some men have all the luck.